# Seven, No More

# Seven, No More

*A Southern Mill Village Family
Moves Up in the World*

*Marlene Rose*

Ivy House
Publishing Group

www.ivyhousebooks.com

*To my loving husband, Levy, for his encouragement
in all my efforts.*

PUBLISHED BY IVY HOUSE PUBLISHING GROUP
5122 Bur Oak Circle, Raleigh, NC 27612
United States of America
919-782-0281
www.ivyhousebooks.com

ISBN: 1-57197-438-5
Library of Congress Control Number: 2004114327

© 2005 Marlene Rose
All rights reserved, which includes the right to reproduce
this book or portions thereof in any form whatsoever except as
provided by the U.S. Copyright Law.

*This is a work of fiction. Names, characters, places, and incidents are either
a product of the author's imagination or are used fictitiously. Any resemblance to actual events or persons, living or dead, is entirely coincidental.*

Printed in the United States of America

# Contents

| | |
|---|---|
| Anna Grace | 1 |
| Anna Grace in Trouble | 8 |
| Raiding the Icebox | 13 |
| In Her Second Year | 16 |
| Ellie Mae | 20 |
| Our Aunt Grace | 25 |
| Food, Fun, and Family | 28 |
| Blackberries and the Fourth | 35 |
| Chick's Café | 41 |
| Shiny Gray Box | 44 |
| School—Sickness—School | 53 |
| War on the Horizon | 59 |
| Our Trip to Newport News | 61 |
| Rationing and Air Raids | 67 |
| The Outhouse | 73 |
| Return to the Mill | 78 |
| Moving | 83 |
| Anna Grace Faces Death | 88 |
| Going to Church | 98 |

| | |
|---|---:|
| Sara Beth | 102 |
| Fishing | 106 |
| Driving Miss Susie | 111 |
| Jim Boy! | 115 |
| A New Job | 127 |
| Mama Goes to the Dentist | 134 |
| Planning for Christmas (Buying Presents) | 138 |
| "One Tree" | 142 |
| Decorating the Tree | 146 |
| Christmas Eve and Christmas Day | 149 |
| After Christmas | 154 |
| Mama's Sickness | 158 |
| New House! New Beginnings! | 161 |

# *Anna Grace*

Moans, groans, screams and more screams, ranting and raving. "I can't push anymore," cried the lively raven-haired girl in the big bed, pulling her long raven hair until she had balls clutched tight in her long, slender fingers.

Screaming so loud in her stark-raving madness, she scared the little girl next door. Into the house Karen ran crying, "Mama, Mama, someone is dying. It must be that pretty lady with the fat tummy next door. I knew she didn't look right."

Finally Dr. Jones arrived. "Tie her hands down or she will be bald-headed before that baby comes. Why, girl, I have never seen such a display of madness in my twenty years of delivering babies. Most young ladies are so pleased to be bringing a little bundle of joy into this world."

But not this girl. She was so self-centered that a little creature might steal some of her attention from others. She was very beautiful and she knew it. For eighteen years she

*Seven, No More*

was the center of attention from her siblings, and now from her nineteen-year-old husband.

Grant you, this world was full of a lot of needy people during the Great Depression. There was not enough food, money, work, or anything else except fatigue and grief from the stress of trying to find food and shelter for the family. Now another person would have to be fed, clothed, and sheltered.

The rich controlled most of the food, clothing, housing, and money. The wealthy owned the cotton patches, cotton mills, tobacco patches, tobacco warehouses, company stores, and even the houses for their workers. No one was considered to be a slave, but there was little time for anything except work. Most everything was controlled by the rich people. Much of the education opportunity was for a select few unless you had enough money to buy your way into the university system. In the working class, by the time a child reached the age of twelve or thirteen years old, their schooling was second to getting the work done in the cotton and tobacco fields. At the ripe age of sixteen years, the young people were sent to work in the cotton mills or tobacco markets. Only a few of these young people were able to continue with their education and find freedom from working in the mill and owing the company store. It took a lot of sacrifice from the parents and extended families to help these young folks stay in school.

The rich people also controlled the company store. Everyone was allowed to charge until payday. If you were a farmer raising cotton or tobacco, you paid up at harvest time. Some of the farmers were tenant farmers, so only half of the crops they raised were theirs; the other half belonged to the owners of the land. Their indebtedness to the company store had to be paid from their half of the crop. Hardly any money was left to start the next year of planting. It was a continuous cycle of borrowing and paying.

By the time the factory workers received their paycheck at the end of the week, their meager wages were used to pay off their indebtedness at the company store. For them also, it was a never-ending cycle of borrowing and paying. The rich got richer, and the poor saw no end to the burdens of their life. No way for them to become free, but there had to be a better way of life for their children.

Here came the screaming, raving, and panting again. In between the screams the mother-to-be could be heard saying, "Take it, take it."

Over and over she continued her wild, mad behavior for what appeared to be hours on end, screaming, "I'm going to die. Can't somebody do something?"

Dr. Jones was giving orders to her mama. "Put some clean water in a kettle; put it on the stove to heat. Get some clean white cloths or rags together. We have to be ready for the birth of this baby when the time comes." All of a sudden the screaming ceased and a big yell came like the kind you feel when you are being taken apart. Out of the madness came a baby. Such a beautiful black-haired girl, but there was no cry.

"Is she alive?" groaned the young mother. "All of this work for a dead baby."

Suddenly the young lady started crying uncontrollably. "She is dead, dead, and she almost killed me too."

All the while, Dr. Jones was busy spanking the baby's little heinie, turning her upside down and slapping her on the heinie again. Suddenly she let out a big screeching yell, the

*Seven, No More*

kind that tells you the world will know about her and her power.

On that hot day in late May came a little raven-haired Taurus who would capture the world with her cunning power, charming personality, and creativity, a girl child to be reckoned with from the first breaths of life. She would hold her subjects in the palm of her little hands.

With hot water in a white enamel basin, Dr. Jones cleaned the little missy and her mama, putting several stitches into her mama's vagina, because that little missy tore her real good. Her dad just cried at the sight of her throwing her arms and legs, peeing on everything under her, but that didn't matter much because she was alive and looked in perfect condition. In her hands, she captured another prisoner; this little raven-haired doll named Anna Grace was a real charmer. Grandpa took her little hand in his big scratchy hand, telling her she was going to be his buddy. Little did he know that her charm had already made him a prisoner. My, my, Anna Grace seemed destined to rock this world with her cunning power, charming personality, and creativity.

With the hardships of the Depression—standing in line for hours to get limited food for their families—Anna Grace brought some joy for a Depression-ridden family: Mama, Daddy, Grandma, and Grandpa were in need of worldly things, but not in need of love.

Everyone had fallen in love with this little missy—Anna Grace. Everyone wanted to do something special for this special child.

Grandma was so busy helping the good Dr. Jones getting the hot water and clean white cloths that she did not have much time for the little missy, but that was fine because Anna Grace would charm this fine lady—Grandma.

*Marlene Rose*

At the time of Anna Grace's birth, her mama, dad, Uncle Clem, Aunt Barb, and Grandma and Grandpa lived together in one of the rented mill houses. With the Great Depression it took all four of the grown-ups working in the cotton mill to make ends meet. A few dollars a day was their earnings, so at the end of the week on payday, the four of them would head to the company store to pay for their groceries, cigarettes, and rent.

Almost everyone smoked cigarettes from the early age of thirteen. Seems like that was one pleasure no one was willing to give up. With another mouth to feed, how were they going to make it? How were they going to spoil this little missy? Would she be spoiled or just loved? Perhaps both, but either way Anna Grace would benefit. From the company-owned shotgun house in the mill village, everyone walked to work. You either worked the morning, evening, or graveyard shift. Anna Grace's parents and grandparents split their shifts so someone was always home with her.

On this beautiful, hot, sweaty day, nearly everyone passed by Anna Grace's house on his or her way to and from work at the cotton mill. They stopped by the little neat house with the pansies crying for rain to see the newest little girl in the village. "Isn't she pretty? How much does she weigh?" said the woman with the big nose and straight black hair pulled into a tight knot; her blue printed apron was pulled tight around her waist, showing the forty-two-inch bust hanging out the top of her blouse and her twenty-inch waist, with her big butt to match her bust. Daddy said she had a figure like a burlesque queen. She wore her hair that way because she was a spinner at the mill, and she could lose her hair if it got caught in one of the spinning machines. That spinning machine might even pull her head off. What a sight that

## Seven, No More

would be: a headless spinner. Anna Grace made up her mind that day she was not going to be a spinner, let alone look like that lady and worry about losing her head.

News of the new baby girl reached all over the mill village by the next shift. That spinning lady must have had a fast tongue for news to spread so fast. Visitors called, but no presents. With this Great Depression, there was no money for presents.

One little lady with a big toothless smile and bright blue eyes brought her a pretty pink-checked blanket made from flour sacks. Sewed with multicolored thread, the blanket was beautiful. As hot as it was, Anna Grace didn't need much covering, but it was real nice that the lady made the blanket just for her.

Mama said Miss Mary Moore was the best sewer in the mill village, and she was pleased that Miss Mary thought of her new little baby girl. Miss Mary, everyone called her, stayed with her parents and took care of them as long as they had lived. She was one of the kindest, gentlest, and most generous persons in the mill village. Now Miss Mary was alone in the house where she grew up. Always considerate, she remembered everyone on special occasions. She never forgot to honor the dead and to congratulate the newlyweds and the new babies. She made most of her presents, and they were always appreciated. Her parents taught her well.

This house where Anna Grace was born was no mansion. When both of the parents worked at the mill, they were entitled to rent a shotgun house with two bedrooms and a toilet on the back porch. Each house had a little kitchen and a small sitting room. In the kitchen was an icebox, a two-burner gas stove with a tiny oven—big enough for ten biscuits—plus two small cabinets made out of metal and painted white with silver handles. All the staple foods were kept in these cabinets. Two cabinets were enough to store their dishes and food.

Anna Grace's family was entitled to a bigger house with three bedrooms and a toilet on the back porch, because they had four people working at the mill.

As an infant Anna Grace slept in the same bedroom with Mama and Daddy. They were afraid they would not hear her cry. Well, they would have heard her cry, no matter where she slept—she would have made sure of that. Truth was, that was the only place for her to sleep.

The first days of Anna Grace's life were pretty normal: drinking, sleeping, and peeing on everything under her.

Many of the mill people came by every day or so to see how much the little missy had grown. Anna Grace would open that toothless mouth and smile. Maybe she liked what she saw, or maybe she was passing gas. Sometimes Anna Grace would pass a little more than gas.

As time passed she grew into the mill village baby. Everyone loved her, and Anna Grace returned that love.

Anna Grace was a special child in a hard Depression mill village. Long, hard hours of work with little money to buy the necessities of life were brightened by the smile and laughter of this raven-haired, black-eyed missy.

# Anna Grace in Trouble

As time passed, Anna Grace grew into a curious little girl, crawling all over the house like a little kitten, exploring her interesting surroundings. One such place was Grandma's dresser; she began pulling everything out of the drawers, and some strange things were in those drawers—shiny, silky things that Mama and Grandma put on their legs.

Next her attention went to the shoes lying on the floor next to the dresser. Anna Grace couldn't walk, so she tried standing in the shoes; they toppled her to the floor, both shoes going in different directions. If she could not walk in them, perhaps she could eat them. As she started to eat the shiny shoes, she threw them across the room and started crying. Those shoes tasted terrible. Some of her food tasted like milk and honey compared to them.

Grandma heard her sobs. She ran to Anna Grace, only to trip over her own black patents that the youngster had been chewing. "That girl is going to cause me to break my leg," Grandma said.

## Marlene Rose

Anna Grace started laughing at Grandma lying on the floor. Looking at Anna Grace laughing, Grandma started laughing too. She laughed so hard that she started crying, soaking her face with tears of love and joy. She grabbed Anna Grace, giving her a big hug.

Anna Grace was ready for more exploring, crawling into the kitchen as fast as her hands and legs would carry her. This was the most interesting room in the house. Everyone liked the table because they were always sitting around it—eating, talking, and laughing.

Anna Grace climbed into one of the cane bottom chairs, then crawled and slid into the middle of the table. She thinks to herself, *Mum, what's that stuff in that jar?* She put her little hands around the jar and put the jar between her legs. She stretched her little hand around the top of the jar like she had seen her daddy do and pulled to loosen it, turning and turning until the top flew off, splashing stuff all over her white-smocked apron.

Finding the top open, she stuck her little hand into the liquid, pulled her hand out, then licked her fingers. *Tastes funny!* She decided to get some things out of the jar to eat. *They must be good, because Grandma eats them all the time.* With her tiny hand she reached inside the jar, feeling a long, green, silky thing. She tried to pull the long, green, silky thing out of the jar, but it just slid through her fingers. She tried again and again; then all of a sudden the green, slippery thing popped out. It was all wet and slimy. Her eyes began to burn, but she had to take a bite of that thing Grandma liked so much. Grandma said, "It is hot, hot but so good." Into her mouth Anna Grace put that long, green, slimy thing, biting hard with her four big teeth. Now it stung and burned, and she started to cry, screaming at the top of her voice. Maybe

*Seven, No More*

the top of the house would come off and the wind will cool her mouth and somehow cool her hot stomach.

Everyone in the house came running, blaming each other for not watching Anna Grace. "Oh, my gracious she has eaten hot pepper," Mama shouted. "She will surely die." Grabbing Anna Grace, they ran as fast as they could to the '37 Ford in the yard. Mama, Daddy, Grandpa, and Grandma all headed to the hospital with Mama holding Anna Grace. She didn't want Anna Grace to die, especially in her arms. Now the hospital was a long ways from the house, but Daddy's driving cut the time in half. He was driving that '37 Ford and talking to Jesus. The distance gave Anna Grace some time to cool her mouth with all the wiping Grandma was doing with a white wet washrag. Later she learned that Grandma only used white washrags because they represented purity. Purity is necessary when you are asking God for something. They were asking God to spare Anna Grace's life, since she was a baby and could not ask God herself.

Now these people were crazy if they thought Anna Grace was going to die. She came here to stay awhile and find out what is in this world, but the hospital visit was necessary to stop the burning in her mouth and stomach. She heard Grandma say that God wasn't finished with Anna Grace yet.

This big fat man without any hair and wearing glasses gave Anna Grace a spoonful of white chalky stuff to swallow. She spit it back at him; he tried again and she spit it back again, but this time all over his white coat. He must have been the doctor or someone learning to be a doctor. He was somebody's boss because he screamed as loud as he could for a nurse. Into the room came running this pretty, white-haired, blue-eyed girl. "Give her the medicine," he said, leaving

## Marlene Rose

the room. The pretty nurse gave Anna Grace a spoonful of that awful white chalky stuff, which she gladly swallowed. She would have taken another spoonful for that pretty, white-haired nurse. After she took the medicine, the doctor returned, saying the most awful thing Anna Grace had ever heard. "If she were my child, I would spank that bottom," but never you mind, he soon fell under the spell of Anna Grace. Her charm captured the hearts of the doctors, nurses, and everyone at the hospital. The pretty, white-haired nurse put Anna Grace into this white wired bed she called a crib. Grandpa had a box in the backyard with wire like that he called a chicken crib, so Anna Grace wondered what was the difference between the two cribs. At the hospital the crib was white, while Grandpa's crib was brown. Maybe the difference is the color between a child's crib and a chicken crib. The pretty nurse started rubbing Anna Grace's legs, saying, "This will relax your muscles," but her muscles didn't hurt. Her mouth was burning. The rubbing made her feel good, and Anna Grace gave her one of her four-tooth smiles. Maybe the rubbing did help the burning mouth and stomach.

All the grown-ups at the hospital thought they knew everything. They were telling Mama and Daddy that Anna Grace behaved like an angel. Anna Grace was sure Mama and Daddy knew the difference between her and an angel.

Into the hospital room Daddy came, saying, "Thank you, Jesus! Thank you, Jesus." Anna Grace wondered what Jesus had to do with her getting better because the doctors and nurses were the people putting that white stuff in her mouth.

On the way home from the hospital, Mama asked Daddy, "Do you think this hospital visit will stop Anna Grace from plundering?"

Daddy replied, "I doubt it. She's a curious child that's

## Seven, No More

interested in everything and everyone." Daddy asked Mama, "Wonder what this child will do with her life?"

Mama replied, "I don't know, but whatever it is, she will create havoc."

Anna Grace could hardly wait to stop crawling; she wanted to take that big step. Every time she moved, someone had arms and hands outstretched, saying, "Walk, walk, walk. You can do it." If they knew she could walk, why were they continuously telling her to walk?

"She will walk when she's ready," Grandma said. Around fourteen months Anna Grace took the big step and never stopped.

# Raiding the Icebox

After the pepper episode you would think someone would have been watching Anna Grace. Uncle Clem was given the task of keeping an eye on her. Anna Grace knew how to con Uncle Clem. He liked the girls. On the coffee table was a magazine with girls all over the front. Accidentally Anna Grace knocked it on the floor. While he was picking it up, he saw all those pretty girls all over the cover. Immediately he sat down on the floor and started reading.

*Now this is my time to raid the icebox,* thought Anna Grace. In order to reach the icebox, she pulled up one of the cane bottom chairs from the kitchen table. Thrilled with excitement she opened the icebox door to find eggs, milk, butter, some green stuff, and leftovers from supper. Not much was left over in this house, but every bite of leftovers was saved. On Fridays Grandma would make soup with the leftovers. The soup was so delicious with salty crackers.

*What else is in this icebox?* Yellow butter. The top of the butter was hard to take off but she was determined, so she

## Seven, No More

pushed and pulled until the lid fell off. Rubbing her fingers across that yellow velvety butter was so satisfying, but licking her fingers was even better. *That butter is some good stuff.* Again she rubbed her fingers across the butter; it had the same smooth taste. Since she was exploring the icebox, she picked up one of those eggs. Anna Grace knew that eggs were good; she ate them most mornings for breakfast. Her little hand could not hold the egg, but the kitchen floor could. Smash, there it went; it looked like the egg needed cooking. Well, maybe she could pick up another egg with her little hand. *The floor got that egg too.*

*Someone is coming.* She knew they would spank her, but it wasn't her fault. The eggs just slipped out of her hand. Aunt Barb took her down from the chair, and then she closed the icebox.

Calmly she spoke, "Honey, let's me and you clean up this mess before someone slides down." Aunt Barb went to find some clean rags to clean the floor. Aunt Barb scrubbed and scrubbed all the egg stuff. Anna Grace tried to help her by walking across the floor to see if anyone could slide down. If she couldn't slide down, no one else could. Boy, was she wrong. Uncle Clem hit the floor with a bang. Did Anna Grace and Aunt Barb ever laugh! His feet must have been like skates that he didn't know how to use. Aunt Barb laughed so hard, she slid down. Anna Grace had to join the fun. All three of them were on the floor with gluey egg stuff on their bottoms. Mama did not smile much; they believed all this egg stuff on the floor would not get a smile from her. Mama was always grouchy with sad eyes. Uncle Clem and Aunt Barb worked hard cleaning the egg stuff while Anna Grace worked hard spreading the gluey egg stuff all over the kitchen floor. The harder they wiped the floor, the more

*Marlene Rose*

Anna Grace spread the egg stuff. All three of them looked like they were ready to be fried; they were already scrambled.

Finally they finished cleaning the floor; it looked like a mirror. All three of them could see themselves, but they did not look so good with egg all over their feet, legs, arms, and clothes. Their feet got most of the egg. After the egg dried on their feet, it was difficult to move them for walking.

Aunt Barb washed Anna Grace's arms and legs and tried to clean her feet with some old rags. After getting Anna Grace clean, Aunt Barb insisted Anna Grace sit in her high chair like a good little girl who had never been in trouble. "Your mama will never know," Aunt Barb kept saying under her breath.

Uncle Clem kept saying out loud, "It's all my fault." It didn't matter whose fault. They had fun.

# In Her Second Year

Some time in the second year of Anna Grace's life, her parents had saved enough money to rent their own shotgun house in the mill village. Leaving Grandma, Grandpa, Uncle Clem, and Aunt Barb made Anna Grace very sad. Both families knew the move would be good for everyone. Grandpa and Grandma had been so wonderful to take the family into their home. Now Uncle Clem and Aunt Barb could have their bedroom again.

The new house had two bedrooms and a toilet on the back porch.

Mama and Daddy must have had more money than Grandpa and Grandma because the family now had a big front porch. The porch reached across the front of the house with a swing big enough for the three of them. On the front porch, attached to the house, Daddy put an American flag that he bought at the five-and-dime store.

In the hot evening time, everyone gathered around on the porches in the village, reading the obituaries or just talking

*Marlene Rose*

with their neighbors. Anna Grace busied herself playing with a little doll someone from a rich family threw into the weekly trash. Her grandpa rescued the doll for his little precious angel. It didn't matter to Anna Grace where the doll came from or who owned the doll before her. Anna Grace gave that doll lots of love. She would chatter to the doll, dressing and undressing her with clothes Mama made from scraps of flour sack fabric left over from Anna Grace's dresses.

Sometimes Miss Mary Moore would make blankets for Anna Grace's baby doll. Miss Mary was such a fine lady. She told Mama that Anna Grace was like a grandchild to her. She appreciated Mama sharing Anna Grace.

Grandpa said it was a pleasure to see Anna Grace so happy; now if only this awful Depression would end or just get better. He was so happy that Mama and Daddy had a place to call home, even though it was rented. Anna Grace heard Mama tell Daddy in her matter-of-fact attitude, "We have plenty of room for the furniture and clothes we have."

All Anna Grace saw her mama wear were two different dresses, a pair of navy canvas shoes, a pair of beautiful shiny black high heels, and some silky things on her legs.

Anna Grace had a Sunday dress and play dresses made from flour sacks, a pair of play shoes, and a pair of black shiny shoes with pearl buttons. These shoes were the most beautiful shoes Anna Grace had ever seen. When the mill village people came by on their way to work, Anna Grace would show them her shiny black shoes.

Without any money Anna Grace didn't know how they bought the shoes; maybe Grandpa pulled them out of the trash like he did her doll. It didn't matter where they came from because now they were hers.

Grandma and Aunt Bessie saved all their flour sacks for

## Seven, No More

Mama to sew clothes for Anna Grace. Aunt Bessie, Daddy's sister, only had boys. She said, "They could wear a pair of jeans until they outgrew them or wore them out."

Occasionally Mama would make the boys a shirt if the patterns were suitable.

With the washboard Mama and Grandma scrubbed the flour sacks clean with water and lye soap. Making the lye soap was a real production that lasted all day. They made enough soap to last several months.

In the backyard Grandma built a fire around the big black kettle to heat the liquid for making the lye soap. Putting lard cut into squares and lye into the hot kettle as the lard started melting, they began stirring the liquid with a big board similar to a boat paddle. It was essential not to get any of the lye on your hands, because the lye would bleach the skin.

After boiling the liquid for hours, the soap was poured on a board to harden and dry. After the soap cooled it was cut into bars. They let the soap set for days before they used it.

In many families of the village, lye soap was used to wash all the clothes. The children would wear their clothes until they were real dirty. Grandma used lye soap to wash the flour sacks for the dresses. After washing the sacks, she would hang them on the line to dry. The clothesline stretched across the backyard for about fifty feet, with clothesline wire attached to two forked-like poles. All the washed clothes were hung there to dry: the aroma from the sun took out most of the lye soap odor. Grandma said it was God's time to clean them. These flour sacks were stiff as boards and would stand straight up like the ones Pete and Sally used for their seesaw.

Pete and Sally were Daddy's younger brother and sister, always telling Anna Grace that when she got bigger she could ride their seesaw. By the time Anna Grace grew big enough to ride that darned seesaw, it would have been used for firewood to heat the house or to burn under the wash pot.

It seems like nothing stayed the same during this Depression except hard work, doing without, and no money. Everyone was doing without and had no money.

Almost every day Pete and Sally would come to play with Anna Grace. Pete would stand Anna Grace on the pump stand, turn the water on, and tell her to dance. Her dress and shoes would be soaked. Sally yelled to Pete, "Stop, she is going to slide down and get hurt. Her mama will wear you out. You know how mean her mama can be. Stop, Pete, stop," cried Sally.

Pete would only listen to Anna Grace's daddy. Because of his second job at the dairy, Daddy was not around until late, and by then Pete and Sally had gone home. Pete enjoyed terrorizing Anna Grace, but she enjoyed his play so much. The more Pete ran the water, the more Anna Grace laughed and danced.

# Ellie Mae

One day the woman with the big nose and straight black hair pulled tight into a knot came by the house. She commented to Mama how fleshy she was getting. As she often did, Mama lost her temper and told the "old biddy" to tend to her own business. Well, she tended to her own business all right. With her fast tongue, everyone on the mill village knew Mama was getting "fleshy," whatever that meant.

Later that fall, when it was cold and the pumpkins were big for Halloween, Mama had another baby girl. Anna Grace was a big sister to this baby girl, Ellie Mae. Anna Grace would teach her everything—especially how to get your way with these big people around her. Everyone was fussing over that baby and saying she was so good and pretty. She was the best baby in the world, not like Anna Grace who was getting into everything. One thing for sure, Anna Grace would teach her how to be a big girl.

With Ellie Mae drawing all the attention, Anna Grace decided it was time for action. Into her bedroom she went,

*Marlene Rose*

pulling a chair from the kitchen table. The chair was painted red with different color flowers painted down the sides. All four chairs at the table were painted different, but this was Anna Grace's favorite chair. Pulling, pushing, and banging the walls; sliding the chair across the room until she reached the chest of drawers; pulling the chair closer to the chest of drawers, she climbed on the chair and pulled the chest over. *Bang, bam, bang*—everything on top landed in the middle of the floor. All the drawers fell out—clothes, sheets, towels—piled scattered on the floor. Everyone came running. Ellie Mae just listened; for the time being Anna Grace had won again.

During the cleanup of the mess, Mama in her frustration said, "If she wasn't so small, I would wear out her bottom."

Grandma replied, "Oh, don't be so hard on her. She is just jealous. For over two years Anna Grace had all the attention. Eventually she will learn to share everyone and everything with her new baby sister. One day the two of them will be best friends."

Like most girls Anna Grace learned at an early age how to get her way. As time passed and Ellie Mae was growing into a toddler, Anna Grace was learning to share more things and people, except Grandma and Grandpa—there was no sharing; neither would she share her black shiny shoes with the white pearl buttons. She had to share her daddy because Mama would tell him, "It's your turn with the young-uns."

Mama was really busy now, working in the mill, sewing for the girls, keeping Daddy's food warm, and getting fleshy again. Every time she got fleshy, another baby would come.

When she got fleshy this time, a baby boy came. Mama was tickled pink.

Anna Grace didn't know why boys were so special. If she

## Seven, No More

had known boys were that special, she might have asked Jesus to make her a boy. Many times she heard Daddy say Jesus knows all things and can do all things. Jesus could have made her a boy; instead he made Anna Grace a girl.

Grandpa was always telling Anna Grace how special she was. Girls can do almost anything. Just take a look at Mama and Grandma; they cook, clean, sew, work at the mill, and have babies. All the mill village people talked about Ellie Mae being smart and good, and Mama agreed. She learned everything from Anna Grace. Now with this brother coming along, Anna Grace didn't know if she wanted to teach him anything. Most of the time Mama was holding and feeding him.

At mealtime Ellie Mae and Anna Grace were put in red wooden high chairs with trays for their food, but not that brother Billy Bob.

It's easy to understand why Ellie Mae was in the high chair with a tray; she always spilled her milk but not her food. She ate her food so fast, waiting for seconds. At the house there were no seconds unless Anna Grace—who was a picky eater—left some for Ellie Mae.

Anna Grace wanted to sit on one of the big chairs, but Mama said, "No way." She knew Anna Grace would get into some mischief. If she had let her sit in that big red chair with flowers painted down the side, Mama might have been surprised how good Anna Grace could be.

Suddenly there was the sound of footsteps outside. "What's that noise?" Mama asked. "Why, it's Grandpa."

Sitting in her high chair, Anna Grace reached for him with outstretched arms and hands. With his big red strong hands he pulled her out of the high chair, lifting her on his big wide shoulders. Anna Grace grabbed his cold, black

*Marlene Rose*

straight hair, giggling. Because his hair was so greasy with Vaseline, her little fingers slid right off. She smelled her hands. Smelled like red apples but not eatable apples. That smell came from Grandpa's hair. *It must be the hair grease he uses to keep his hair black and shiny.* It didn't matter where the odor came from—his hair or the hair grease. It smelled good enough to eat.

"Do you know where we are going?" Grandpa asked. "We are going to Mr. Mac's store for candy."

Off to Mr. Mac's store, Anna Grace riding on Grandpa's big wide shoulders, leaving Ellie Mae crying. Grandpa said to Ellie Mae, "We will bring you some candy. Just stop crying and be a good girl for your mama."

As the two entered the store, Mr. Mac called out, "How is my girl today?"

Anna Grace just smiled, showing him her new teeth. She had come to get a bag of candy for herself. Holding tight in her hand, she had a big piece of money for Mr. Mac. She handed him what Grandpa said was a nickel. On the counter was a big, big jar full of peppermint sticks, molasses Mary Janes, orange slices, and sticky gummy bears. Into the big round jar, she put her little hand, grabbing all that little hand could hold, stuffing the candy into her brown bag. Anna Grace wanted to get another handful for Ellie Mae, but Grandpa said, "You need to share your candy with her."

If Anna Grace shared her candy with Ellie Mae, she would get two pieces of orange slices. Ellie Mae didn't have but four teeth and she couldn't eat much candy. Orange slices and gummy bears are pretty good on your gums without many teeth. Anna Grace had strong teeth; she just didn't have many. Anna Grace liked the Mary Janes best because the

*Seven, No More*

candy would stick to your teeth and you could chew longer, getting all the sugar out of the candy.

With a bag full of candy and a mouth full of Mary Janes, Grandpa and Anna Grace started home. Anna Grace remembered what Mama told her time and again: "If you keep eating candy, all of your teeth will fall out."

Every day Anna Grace looked to see if her teeth were falling out; instead her teeth just multiplied. Every time she looked, more teeth were coming. Anna Grace didn't believe Mama knew very much about losing teeth. All the way home she held tight to Grandpa's hair and her sack of candy. It was good that Billy Bob didn't have teeth, because sharing with Ellie Mae was enough.

# Our Aunt Grace

Anna Grace was glad she was born first; she got the prettiest and best name. Anna Grace was named for Aunt Grace, the gum-eating orange slice lady in the family. Standing four feet, ten inches, weighing ninety pounds soaking wet, she was a bit feisty for her ninety years. Tiny gray curls around her head with a toothless smile every now and then, if you caught her without her false teeth. Those teeth might be in a jarful of water in the kitchen soaking to get clean. With or without teeth she could gum those orange slices. "She gums everything," Grandpa says of his older sister. Everybody had a sister, even Anna Grace.

Even at her age Aunt Grace could play that piano and sing. Grandma said, "Aunt Grace had a sharp tongue, and that's where Mama inherited her sharp tongue." Aunt Grace demanded much from her husband.

Often you could hear her tell Uncle Will, "Old Man, you are so slow molasses would freeze on you."

Anna Grace liked visiting Aunt Grace and Uncle Will

## Seven, No More

because Aunt Grace always had orange slices for her. Even though the piano was missing some ivories, Aunt Grace could play that piano and sing. At the top of their voices Aunt Grace and Anna Grace would sing strong and loud. Aunt Grace would play the piano, her gray curly head bobbing and her fanny reeling on that red, round, velvet-covered stool keeping in tune with the music.

Even though her sight was dim, with her music and her cat named Salty, Aunt Grace was a delight to be around. Salty was a black and white barn tomcat. When Aunt Grace would sing, he would roll his eyes, turn his ears toward the music, and purr. Anna Grace must have inherited her love for cats from Aunt Grace. Must be a generational thing; Mama inherited her sharp tongue and Anna Grace her love for cats from Aunt Grace. Always a loving and generous person, Aunt Grace praised Mama for her sewing talent and rearing such delightful children.

Even with stiff flour sacks she made the most beautiful dresses. Mama could really sew. At church everyone thought the girls were wearing crinolines by the way their skirts stood out. Anna Grace's dresses always had a full gathered skirt and sash because people said she looked like a poor orphan being so thin, but not that Ellie Mae. She had plenty of meat on her bones. Most likely she ate Anna Grace's food, except the candy. Most always the two girls had a short bob haircut with big hair bows to match. Grandma said cutting the girls' hair short would thicken it and give it lots of body.

Even though money was scarce, Mama and Grandma made sure their little girls looked and behaved beautifully. The two ladies with their creativity and hard work made Anna Grace and Ellie Mae look like a million.

## Marlene Rose

With working at the mill, sewing for Anna Grace and Ellie Mae, cooking, and taking care of the family, Mama had time to get fat again. Every time mama got fat, another baby would come. Another mouth to feed, and during this Depression this was not easy. Food and money were hard to come by, but somehow with all the hard work, love, and togetherness, the family managed.

# Food, Fun, and Family

After Daddy worked the first shift at the cotton mill, he went to his second job at Mr. Collins's dairy farm. Part of the benefit was fresh eggs, milk, and butter for the family. Occasionally Mrs. Collins would send home with Daddy a freshly made apple pie or some fruit cobbler. Anna Grace loved her blackberry pie, made with fresh blackberries and crisp pie shells. They were good enough to eat by themselves.

Mr. and Mrs. Collins were elderly without children of their own; they treated Daddy like he was their son, and his children like their grandchildren. It was a blessing to have Daddy work for them, and for the Collinses to be an extended family.

Every morning Mr. Collins, walking with a cane, would climb on his buggy loaded with fresh milk, butter, eggs, and cream to deliver to the market in town for the rich people to buy.

After working at the mill and the dairy, Daddy would come home tired and hungry. Always Mama had a good meal

*Marlene Rose*

prepared for the family. Most of the food came from the little garden she planted in the backyard, except the butter, milk, and eggs that Mrs. Collins sent. The family had some good food—corn on the cob with butter, green beans, tomatoes, cucumbers, okra, and some good homemade biscuits. All Mama bought from the company store was flour, sugar, corn meal, molasses, and Daddy's cigarettes. Many times Mama and Daddy talked about getting out of the Depression: being free from the bondage of living daily on the edge. The garden with the fresh vegetables and milk, eggs, and butter from the dairy had a big impact on the money in the family. Mama's sewing also contributed a lot toward reaching freedom. The wages at the mill and dairy were very meager. During this Depression everything the two of them did helped toward freedom from debt. Even after Daddy worked twelve hours every day, he had time for his family. After bathing, eating, and resting a little while, it was time for his children. Even though Anna Grace was very young, she knew her daddy was a special person. Reading the Bible and singing Sunday school songs were very special to the three children. Every time Daddy would tell the story about Moses rolling back the waters so all Israel's prisoners could go free from the slavery of Egypt to another land that God promised, Anna Grace would ask the same question: "Why are they prisoners? Why didn't God set them free?" Then Daddy would explain over and over again that God set them free through Moses. Moses, following God's instructions on the method to set the children of Israel free, acted in obedience. When the children of Israel gathered at the Red Sea, Moses waved a stick, the waters parted, and the children of Israel passed into freedom. That was not the end of the story; the waters came together again, drowning the

*Seven, No More*

mean Egyptian soldiers. Daddy would say, "If you are obedient and listen to God talking to you in your heart, you would always be free." So why were so many people living in bondage during this Depression? Were they not obedient to God? Anna Grace liked the Bible stories Daddy read to her, Ellie Mae, and Billy Bob.

The prayer time was very special. The three children would pray for everyone. Always Anna Grace would pray for Grandma, Grandpa, Daddy, and Mama last. Mama didn't need as much prayer as the rest of the family because she said she knew Jesus. Anna Grace wondered when she met him, because she didn't remember him coming to their house. One day Anna Grace asked Mama how she knew Jesus, and much to her surprise Mama said, "He is in my heart."

Anna Grace was only four years old and very confused. "How can Jesus live in your heart?" she asked Daddy.

He had the answer, "Jesus lives in our hearts through his spirit. Just like the air we breathe, we cannot see it but it is there. We see the leaves on the trees moving. We feel the breeze, but we cannot see it." Daddy could explain anything so even a four-year-old could understand.

Mama was always cooking, cleaning, and sewing. In order to keep expenses down, Mama made all the clothes. With three children to feed and clothe, she did everything she could to help the family.

On one occasion while shopping for shoes and socks (that was one thing Mama couldn't make) at the local department store (which was a company store), Mama and Daddy lined the three children into chairs for Mr. Barbour to fit their feet. Mr. Barbour was a kind, soft-spoken, balding man who just happened to be a genius; he knew how to fit

*Marlene Rose*

their feet perfect. Every spring and fall the family visited him and the company store for shoes and socks.

"These children are so well behaved. Let me give them a lollipop," said Mr. Barbour. That was good candy.

Sweets were a real treat at the house. "With too much candy," Daddy said, "your teeth will rot and fall out." Daddy did not want to see a snaggled-tooth smile. Jack-o-lanterns were just for Halloween.

Sometimes the children walked with Daddy to Mr. Mac's store to buy oatmeal. Mama always said, "Good food for your breakfast." With milk, oatmeal was nearly a perfect food for growing strong bodies. Billy Bob, Ellie Mae, and Anna Grace grew into big and strong children. It must have been filled with brain power, because Billy Bob sure was smart. He would gobble that gritty stuff like it was chocolate candy. Anna Grace ate enough to keep from starving. Times were hard at the house, but the family was fortunate to move from the mill village into town across from the town water tank. One more step to freedom from the clutches of the mill and the company store.

Uncle Clem joined the United States Army; Aunt Barb married her nineteen-year-old boyfriend. The United States Army offered a lot of hope for the future. Each soldier received a check for service, plus his family received a supplement check. With this little extra money for his wife, Aunt Barb's husband joined the United States Army: she continued to work at the mill. Both Uncle Clem and Aunt Barb's husband wanted more for their life and family than working in the mill and owing their life to the company store.

Aunt Barb would dream of fine clothes for herself and a better education for their children when they had them. Likewise Aunt Barb's husband wanted the same things. After

*Seven, No More*

helping with Anna Grace, though, Aunt Barb could have decided she had enough of children.

Little by little, Aunt Barb was freeing herself from the company store. Maybe freedom was on its way!

It was a great day when the family moved from the mill village into town. The house had three bedrooms, a kitchen with a four-burner gas stove, icebox, and table with four painted chairs. They needed three more chairs and a bigger table; Grandpa went looking in the rich people's trash every week. After several weeks of looking, he added four more chairs, which Daddy painted multicolored to blend with what they had. Sunday was the only time everyone ate together; they worked six days a week on different shifts. Daddy made a table out of scrap wood for the children and painted it red to coordinate with the multicolored chairs.

The setting room had worn-out chair bottoms that Daddy covered with odd pieces of wood so the children would not fall through the bottoms. The sofa was red plastic; and red plastic flowers from the five-and-dime store were on the coffee table that Daddy made. Anna Grace believed everyone bought the same kind of flowers; every house she went had the same red plastic flowers. They had the most disgusting odor about them; you could throw up without sticking your finger down your throat. In front of the red plastic couch was a low square table made from drink cartons and an old piece of junk wood from the wood yard. Daddy could make anything out of wood scraps. Ellie Mae, Billy Bob, and Anna Grace would kneel by the table, play cards, and color or draw with broken crayons. Most likely Billy Bob broke them; he destroyed everything he touched. Sometimes the three of them would make up stories and tell them. Anna

*Marlene Rose*

Grace knew her stories were the best and most interesting because she was older; she had experienced more.

All of the dishes were mismatched except some Lord's Supper plates. The only time they used these plates was when the preacher came to dinner after preaching Sunday. The family did not have the finest dishes or fabulous foods, but they shared what they had; the Lord blessed them. Anna Grace thought Mama might have wanted the preacher to see how religious the family was by using those plates.

Mama was getting fat again; by now Anna Grace figured that meant another baby. A new house and a new baby coming. The house would be full before long, because she was really fat. Anna Grace's birthday was next Monday; she hoped that baby didn't come on her big six-year-old birthday. She didn't want to share that birthday with anyone, especially a new baby getting all the attention. On that big birthday Grandma made her a big chocolate cake with six pink candles. Grandma brought white ice cream; Aunt Barb came with a present wrapped in white paper with a pink paper bow. Aunt Barb was getting fat too. Could she be going to have a baby? Daddy said Aunt Barb was eating too much candy; Mama must be eating too much candy with her big tummy. Before they knew it, all the chocolate cake and the ice cream were gone. Everyone had chocolate cake and white ice cream on them: it was turning Anna Grace's pink birthday dress into pink, white, and black polka dots. Ellie Mae cried because she didn't have a present. Feeling sad for her, Anna Grace let her open a present. Before Anna Grace knew what happened Ellie Mae was eating the chocolate candy Aunt Barb brought her. Aunt Barb knew exactly what Anna Grace liked: chocolate candy! If there was anything Anna Grace liked more, it was more chocolate candy.

## Seven, No More

Billy Bob started crying because he didn't have a present. "Hey, everyone, it's my birthday," shouted Anna Grace.

No one noticed Anna Grace because they were trying to stop the crybabies. Busy as always Anna Grace picked up the cake plates, one by one throwing them into the dishpan on the kitchen counter. As each plate hit one another, they spattered glass everywhere. Mama started screaming for Anna Grace to stop. She stopped, but not until all the plates were broken.

Oh, my—what a birthday!

# Blackberries and the Fourth

The next morning Anna Grace went with Mama, Daddy, and Ellie Mae to pick blackberries for Sunday dinner. Grandma stayed behind with Billy Bob: he would eat all the berries they picked. Since blackberry pie was Mama's favorite dessert, Grandma was going to make her one before the baby came.

Just as they were starting to pick the blackberries, something moved in the bushes. Without looking, Ellie Mae started running, but she stopped when Mama screamed, "Run, run, girls. Run for your life! There is a big black snake in the brush looking straight at me. We are in his territory and getting his berries, but not for long. He can have those berries and everything else in those bushes."

Ellie Mae and Anna Grace ran so fast that their feet left the ground, and Mama was right behind them, carrying her berries and screaming. Everyone certainly hoped that all that running didn't speed Mama's delivery. Ellie Mae and Anna Grace threw their buckets in the bushes at the snake. Daddy

## Seven, No More

stayed behind looking for the snake, which was long gone. He was probably more afraid than the family was. Off to the house they went with enough blackberries for one pie. Mr. Snake got the other bucket of berries. Thinking out aloud, Ellie Mae said, "I will think of that snake every time I see a blackberry."

Grandma was furious with Mama and Daddy. She told Daddy, "You should have stopped her from picking berries in her condition. That new baby will be marked with a snake symbol for sure. I hope not on the face. That would be a constant reminder of your blackberry picking. Mama is hardheaded. She never listens to anyone."

In early July on a hot, humid Saturday morning, Mama started crying, holding on to her stomach. The pains were sharp and fast, coming every fifteen minutes apart. According to Grandma she was getting ready for her delivery. She could have that baby before sundown. To Anna Grace that seemed like a long time for Mama to have pains. Could the running from the snake cause some of the pains?

Being a holiday weekend, everyone was down at the mill celebrating—with games, rides, hot dogs, soft drinks, and beer. The owners of the mill threw a big carnival for their workers on the July Fourth Independence Day weekend every year. It was a fun time for everyone—young and old. It looked like the family would miss the carnival this year.

Little children were running around wild, screaming, playing tag, and riding the carousel. All the painted animals on the carousel were turning around with the music and the children.

All the grown-up women were keeping their eyes on the little ones. It was great for the kids to have fun riding the carousel, playing tag, or running around screaming, but they

*Marlene Rose*

didn't want anyone to get hurt. It probably was a good thing Billy Bob wasn't there; he would make sure someone was injured. Billy Bob and Pete knew how to cause enough havoc that someone would feel pain around them.

Teenaged boys were climbing the greased pole to bring down the American flag. As they climbed a few feet, they would slide back down the pole. Then they would try again until someone won. After about a dozen tries, Pete made it. He brought down the flag and received his reward of a one-hundred-dollar bill. What would he do with that kind of money? "Spend it."

The teenaged girls were running the sack race, screaming for their friends and booing the boys who wanted to race, but this was a girl's race. Sally tried, but she ended last. She would never hear the end of this from Pete. Always bragging, Pete knew he could do anything. Maybe after winning the money from climbing the greased pole, he would leave Sally alone.

The men were playing horseshoes, drinking cold beer, smoking cigarettes, and cussing. Apparently that was what men do at carnivals. If Daddy and Grandpa had been there, they would be doing those things too.

Mr. Chick was serving his famous hot dogs along with cold drinks and cold beers for the men. Cold water tasted good in this ninety-six-degree temperature! Daddy and Grandpa would certainly have enjoyed one of his hot dogs and cold beers, but they were elsewhere.

Daddy sent Aunt Barb to find Dr. Jones because Mama was getting ready for delivery. No one else could go to the carnival, not even Aunt Barb. For the kids, going home with Aunt Barb could have been more fun than the carnival!

Moving about the kitchen, Grandma filled a big kettle

with water, setting it on the stove to boil. With all the summer heat, the house was so hot that the family could hardly stand it. All the windows and doors are open to let the breezes and bugs inside. The breeze seemed to be hotter than usual. The bugs were not even flying. Sweat was running down Grandma's face as she searched for clean white rags. With stinking antiseptic soap, she cleaned the white enamel washbasin for Dr. Jones.

Every night they used that basin for sponge baths; it should have been clean because Mama made sure everything was clean for her children. The only time the children took a whole bath and washed their hair was Saturdays. This Saturday would be different, because a new baby was coming. Everyone's bath time would have to wait for another Saturday. On most Saturdays Mama would heat the water in that big black kettle on the stove and fill the galvanized tub with warm water for bathing. Using Ivory soap and a white washcloth, Anna Grace got to bathe first. Even on the hottest days, the warm water felt so good and clean. Ellie Mae would bathe next, then Billy Bob last. Would you believe Billy Bob always peed in the water? Mama said that was just like a boy and she didn't know what she would do if she had another boy, but she would soon find out. Another boy would be just like Billy Bob. He would pee on everything.

In short time Aunt Barb came back and gathered Ellie Mae, Billy Bob, and Anna Grace to take them to her house. The three really liked going to Aunt Barb's house because she let them do about anything, even empty her candy dishes.

The sitting room had some red plastic roses that nearly every house in the mill village had. The odor of those flowers would make a dead man sick. According to Daddy, Aunt

*Marlene Rose*

Barb was on the heavy side. She had not always been that way. Because she was lonely for her husband she ate all the time. He was somewhere in the big war fighting Hitler and his crowd. Aunt Barb had candy in every dish. The children's little hands were busy grabbing and eating all the candy they could stuff in their mouths. Anna Grace wondered why she had so much candy if that is how she got fat. After taking care of three little people, she would be minus some candy. Anna Grace asked Aunt Barb why Dr. Jones was needed for the delivery. She explained that the delivery would bring a baby girl or baby boy, and that Mama needed Dr. Jones to help her.

"Dear Jesus, please, we do not want another boy to pee on everything," Anna Grace prayed under her breath.

Aunt Barb's house was so hot you could fry an egg without turning on the stove. All the doors and windows were closed and locked because she was alone and afraid. She imagined someone breaking into her house and hurting her. It would take a strong and smart person a long time to break into her house.

Mama said Aunt Barb could come and live with her, but Aunt Barb couldn't deal with Mama's ill temper. Not many people could, but they tolerated Mama because she was so charitable. She was always inviting people to stay overnight, even the honeymoon couples—like the house was a hotel. No one paid to stay because they didn't have any money. Mama would do almost anything for someone in trouble. She would feed them and find them somewhere in the house to sleep.

Late in the evening, Daddy came to take the children home. Gently he gathered the family around him and told them that Mama had a baby girl. The girls thanked goodness

## Seven, No More

that baby was not a boy! With the baby girl, they had four children in the family.

After arriving home, Daddy brought the family into Mama's bedroom to see her and the new baby. Reaching into the bed, he picked up the newest member of the family. She was the most beautiful baby the children had ever seen. She had long black hair stuck to her head and a fat wrinkled face with a tiny nose. Boy, could she cry! When she opened her mouth crying, no teeth could be seen. Anna Grace wanted to hold the baby girl first. Seeing the excitement in her eyes, Daddy handed the baby girl to Anna Grace, saying, "What do we name her?"

Almost instantly Anna Grace replied, "Lilly Lee."

"Why, that is a beautiful name," both he and Mama replied. So the baby girl was named Lilly Lee.

All the children in the family had double names because Grandma said that was a Southern tradition, being that they lived in the Deep South.

# Chick's Café

On most Saturdays, Grandpa and Daddy would let Anna Grace go with them downtown. One of the places they visited was Chick's Café. The café was a small place in the middle of town with red and green neon signs advertising hot dogs and cold draft beer by Miller. It was a mainstay in this small mill town. To locate the men in town on Saturdays, you would go to Chick's Café. In Anna Grace's eyes, the café was big, with a bar up front and tables in the main part of the room. The stools at the bar were covered in red-and-black-checkered man-made leather. Around the walls were wooden booths painted black with the seats covered in the same red and black man-made leather. In the middle of the room were four tables, each table painted black with four chairs painted black. Their cushions were red man-made leather. On each table were black pepper and salt shakers, a mustard jar, and a catsup bottle; the back of the bar was a fountain for draft beer and soft drinks. Hanging on the walls were pictures of cowboys and Indians. Behind the bar was the owner,

## Seven, No More

Mr. Chick, a fat man with black greasy hair. He had a mustache that turned up on the ends, with a big fat tummy covered by a white apron tied in front of that tummy. Someone said he was from another land, but he made the best hot dogs in the world. Those people must have been crazy to let him leave their land. Most of the time, Grandpa and Daddy would eat hot dogs and drink cold beer.

After payday on Fridays, the workers at the mill had enough money to eat at Chick's Café. They could hardly wait to taste his good hot dogs and cold beer. On Saturday morning the café would be full of men from the mill village. Many of them came for one of his hot dogs and a cold beer and to play that lively jukebox with Roy Rogers and Gene Autry records. Anna Grace would eat a hot dog and drink a glass of black drink with a straw perched on one of the stools at the bar.

The men would drink and talk about hard times and Adolf Hitler. Much was going on in Eastern Europe with Adolf Hitler and his Nazi Party. Hitler was trying to gain control of Europe and spread his theory of socialism to the entire world. Hitler already had the Germans convinced that they were a superior race. Many of the men at the café were afraid that the United States would be drawn into the European war.

On one Saturday, as Grandpa, Daddy, and Anna Grace were leaving the house, Mama said to Daddy, "Don't you be drinking any of that beer today, or Anna Grace will tell on you." Anna Grace had been trained to be the spy.

Off the group headed to Chick's Café; the place was full of Grandpa's and Daddy's buddies from the mill. Picking her up, Grandpa sat Anna Grace on a round turning stool. Next he ordered her a hot dog and a black drink. Mr. Chick brought them to Anna Grace. With her red and black stool turning, Anna Grace struggled to eat the hot dog and drink the black drink without spilling it. As she was turning around, she saw the pretty lady bring Daddy and Grandpa their hot dog and a glass of beer. That's not all she brought; she also put a full pitcher of beer in front of them. Anna Grace looked at the pitcher of beer and the both of them, while listening to Roy Rogers and the Sons of the Pioneers sing "Happy Trails."

Anna Grace said, "Let me taste that beer, or I will tell Mama on both of you."

The jukebox stopped and the whole café came to a complete hush, waiting to see what was going to happen. One of the men from the mill thought Anna Grace was going to be spanked, but his buddy spoke up. "He knows better than to spank her. The whole family will get him."

Grandpa and Daddy looked red and angry, but Anna Grace didn't care. She got her way, and she got to taste that awful beer. Everyone was quiet as they sat and ate the hot dogs, then drank their beer and went home. No one played the jukebox. Every one was content to sit and quietly hope for another outburst from Anna Grace.

# Shiny Gray Box

On a hot Friday August morning, Mr. Chick from the café drove up in front of the house. His big black car with four doors opened to let Grandpa and Grandma get inside. Grandpa was going to the hospital. Mr. Chick must have been a real good friend to come and take Grandpa to the hospital. Everyone was crying, including Anna Grace; she wanted to go with him. Usually she went about everywhere Grandpa went, but not this time. Mama was crying so loud, saying he won't come back. For sure he would come back. Grandpa was always there.

Three days later he came back in another big black car. The back of the long black car opened, and two men carefully wheeled out a shiny gray box. Toward the front porch they wheeled the gray shiny box with the top securely tight, so whatever was in that box did not fall out. One of the men told Grandma that the body was ready for viewing. Anna Grace watched close by as the two men wheeled the shiny gray box into the sitting room. *That is why Mama was cleaning and crying so much,* Anna Grace thought, *because they had company in that box.* At both ends of the box were latches, and the two men carrying the shiny gray box started unlatching the opening of the box. Grandma started crying and wailing at the top of her voice along with Mama, her sister, and her brother. Everyone was crying, even Anna Grace and Ellie Mae. There was something terrible going on inside that box.

Finally Daddy picked Anna Grace up and said, "Do you want to see Grandpa?"

"You know I do," she said. Holding Anna Grace up to the shiny gray box, she saw her Grandpa asleep. "Wake up, wake up, Grandpa," Anna Grace called, and everyone cried louder.

Holding Anna Grace tight, Daddy said, "Grandpa has gone to heaven to be with Jesus. He has gone to sleep forever so he can be with Jesus in heaven."

At that very moment Anna Grace wanted to go to heaven to be with Grandpa and Jesus. "Just remember Grandpa loved you a lot and one day we can go to be with him," said Daddy.

How can a six-year-old understand what that means? Lots of people were coming to see what was in that shiny gray box that they called a coffin. Some cried; some told him how good he looked; others told the family he was through with suffering. From the mill village came the old biddy that lived across the street. With her sad long face and fast tongue, she told Grandma she would set up with the body. With so many people around, Mama was careful with her own tongue. She didn't want to give the old biddy something to talk about.

At that time everybody was busy looking inside the shiny gray box and talking among themselves. No one was look-

*Seven, No More*

ing after Anna Grace. She crawled among the crowd and stretched out on the floor under the shiny gray box, crying, "Why didn't Jesus take someone else and leave my grandpa?" She cried louder and louder until she thought she was going to throw up. After what seemed like a long time, Daddy saw Anna Grace, picked her up, and carried her to the kitchen. He tried to calm her by offering her some of Miss Mary Moore's chocolate cake and Mama's sweet ice tea. Mama made the best sweet ice tea in the world. During this sad time of mourning, Miss Mary Moore and some other women from the Freewill Baptist Church down the street from their house brought fried chicken, barbecue, potato salad, chocolate cake, and all kinds of pies for the family and friends to eat. Anna Grace loved chocolate cake and sweet ice tea, but not this time. Some things are more important than chocolate cake and sweet ice tea, and that shiny gray box carrying Grandpa was one of those things. People were everywhere, always patting Anna Grace on the head, saying, "That fellow sure loved you." Anna Grace thought, *If he loved me so much, why did he leave without me?* She went with Grandpa everywhere, but not this time. One old lady had the nerve to say that Anna Grace looked just like him. She must have needed glasses, because Anna Grace looked just like her daddy.

People were coming from everywhere to view Grandpa and visit the family. Grandpa had lots of friends, even as far away as Newport News, Virginia. One of Grandpa's friends said it took him all day driving from Williamsburg, but he would not miss this funeral for the world. Most people were dressed up in black clothes. Daddy said black was the right color to wear at funerals. Black was the right color for mourning, and these people were mourning. No one knew

*Marlene Rose*

Grandpa had so many friends. *Were they really his friends,* some of them thought, *or were they here for the food and drinks?*

Anna Grace had never seen so many dressed-up people. "What am I going to wear?" She didn't have a black dress. Mama said children did not go to funerals, but Anna Grace wanted to go to see what was going to happen with her Grandpa. Were the two men going to open the shiny gray box and let him fly to heaven like a bird? Grandma always said Grandpa needed wings like a duck needs water. Mama and Grandma were fussing big-time about Anna Grace going to the funeral. Mama said, "No, she can't go," but Grandma said, "Anna Grace is going to the funeral and that's that." Grandma was now the family boss since Grandpa was leaving to go to heaven, and if Anna Grace wanted to go to the funeral, there was no reason that she shouldn't go. After the fussing, when things settled, Grandma walked downtown to Whitley's Clothiers to purchase a white dress and white shoes for Anna Grace. Her little Anna Grace was going to look pretty for Grandpa's funeral. When Grandma returned from shopping, she found Anna Grace sleeping under the shiny gray box that was holding Grandpa.

With tears running down her checks, Grandma called Anna Grace. "Come see what you are going to wear to Grandpa's funeral."

"Mama said I couldn't go to the funeral," replied Anna Grace.

"You will go if I say you can. I am the boss," answered Grandma. Grandma managed a smile through her tears as she dressed Anna Grace in her white dress and shoes to wear to the funeral.

Lots of people gathered outside, waiting for the family to get in the family car before they went to the funeral. At the

*Seven, No More*

funeral were a lot of people Anna Grace did not know—all dressed in black except Anna Grace, who wore white for purity. Some man with a big stomach and black pencil mustache dressed in a black suit gathered the family in line like they were going to the school bathroom. Anna Grace touched the sleeve of the big man with the pencil mustache. He looked down at her with sad droopy eyes and asked, "What do you want, little lady?"

At that moment Anna Grace felt her heart jumping and panting. She was scared almost to death, too scared to answer him. So he asked her again what she wanted, with his sad droopy eyes settling on her. By this time Anna Grace was feeling a little confident in herself. "I want to be first in line because I am the smallest," she said in a matter-of-fact voice.

He just shook his head no. Anna Grace saw those sad droopy eyes become mean. At that moment, she knew it would be a real task to get her way with this grouch, but Anna Grace had confidence she could do it. Anna Grace walked up to Grandma, put her little hand in hers, and Grandma grasped her little hand so tight that Anna Grace held on for dear life. In her mind, she knew Grandma would approve of her being first in line. No sad droopy-eyed man could stop that. Grandma was the boss in the family, and Anna Grace was her pride and joy. Anna Grace was the assistant to the boss, so you know who was first in line: Anna Grace!

Outside the First Freewill Baptist Church, the family lined up to march behind the shiny gray box. Anna Grace was first, with Grandma holding her tiny hand so tight that it turned white as her dress. After them came Uncle Tom with his wife, Susie. Uncle Tom was Mama's older brother; he lived in Birmingham, Alabama. He worked in a cotton mill—not much different than the family's, just in another town. Grandpa used to say, "You can't escape the mill and its way of life by just changing mill villages. You have to change your environment." That's what Mama and Daddy are trying to do.

Next came Uncle Clem and his lover Ella Frazier, who Mama said was the town tramp. He could certainly do better since he had more to offer, being a soldier in the United States Army.

Following Uncle Clem was Aunt Barb and her husband Jim—also home from the United States Army. After he returned to the base, he was scheduled for duty in Europe. Aunt Barb was upset about his new duty assignment. He kept telling her, "Don't worry about me. I will come back."

Last in line were Mama and Daddy. No children except Anna Grace. "How did that little brat arrange that?" Mama asked Daddy.

He told her, "Be quiet and don't start a fuss here. You know she can charm the horns off a billy goat."

To Anna Grace that sounded like fun, but what would she do with billy goat horns—blow them? Everyone was sitting still, listening to Miss Mattie Hall sing "Shall We Gather at the River?" Anna Grace thought, *Why in this world are we going to gather at the river?* In Anna Grace's thinking, it meant that Grandpa would have to fly over the water on his way to heaven. *What if his wings didn't work, and he fell in the water? Would he still go to heaven?* After Mrs. Mattie Hall finished singing, the preacher got up and started talking about Grandpa. He talked about all the good things Grandpa did and how good a person he was. He never mentioned Grandpa's love for hot dogs and cold beer at Chick's Café. Preacher Tom and Grandma didn't want everyone to know

*Seven, No More*

about Grandpa's vice for hot dogs and cold beer; that was just for the family. Boy oh boy, Anna Grace knew how he loved his cold beer and hot dogs. At that moment she thought that the people at Chick's Café had lost one of their best customers. She was sure Daddy would miss those Saturday outings with Grandpa. Anna Grace would miss them too. After Preacher Tom finished telling how good, loving, and giving a person that Grandpa was, he prayed and sat down.

Then it was time for Miss Mattie Hall to sing again. Grandpa liked to hear her sing "Amazing Grace." Anna Grace helped her with the singing until everyone rolled their eyes toward Anna Grace, and Grandma shook her head no. Immediately Anna Grace hushed her singing. Maybe she was singing off-key or everyone was jealous because they did not know the song; whatever the reason she stopped singing. Anna Grace learned the song at the little holiness church by the railroad tracks. The church was a tiny building with a potbelly stove in the winter. In the hot summer all the windows were open so the neighbors got to listen to the beautiful singing. Anna Grace's Preacher Jim said everyone could receive amazing grace from Jesus, so why did these people not sing this song? After Miss Mattie Hall finished singing, Preacher Tom prayed again and sat down.

Then Preacher Jim, Mama and Daddy's preacher, read the Bible, Psalm 23:

> *The Lord is my shepherd; I shall not want. He maketh me to lie down in green pastures: He leadeth me beside the still waters. He restoreth my soul: He leadeth me in the paths of righteousness for his name's sake. Yea, though I walk through the valley of the shadow of death, I will fear no evil: for thou art with me; thy rod and thy staff they comfort me. Thou preparest a table before me in the presence of mine*

## Marlene Rose

*enemies: thou anointest my head with oil; my cup runneth over. Surely goodness and mercy shall follow me all the days of my life: and I will dwell in the house of the Lord forever.*

After reading the Bible, he prayed for God to bless everyone in their daily living and to give them peace in their hearts and love for each other. He probably knew there was a family feud between the brothers and sisters. Grandma said, "God gives preachers the anointing to know what's happening in families and church." Mama and her siblings were always fussing about something.

Grandma said, "It was pure jealously and envy; one sibling was prettier, smarter, more likeable than another or just being mean." Even at Grandpa's funeral they continued fuming and fussing. After the prayer, everyone lined up behind the shiny gray box, with the sad droopy-eyed, fat, grouchy man leading the way to the big hole in the grassy knoll on the hill behind the church. Holding Grandma's hand tight, Anna Grace walked behind Mr. Grouch, and she could see a green tent with chairs at the grassy knoll. Leading Grandma and Anna Grace, Mr. Grouch seated them side by side, holding each other's hand. When Anna Grace looked at Grandma's face, she could see tears and sadness. Tears were running down her cheeks and on her black dress. Her heart was full of sadness, and Anna Grace felt the sadness too. There was a lot of crying, and then Mr. Grouch with his sad droopy eyes took Grandma by the arm, leading her to the shiny gray box. Anna Grace was right behind her with Mr. Grouch looking at her with those angry eyes. The top of the shiny gray box was open. Grandma looked inside and started crying. Anna Grace stood on her tiptoes, held on to the side of the box, and peeped inside. Much to her surprise, Grandpa was still there. Maybe they opened the box so he could fly

*Seven, No More*

up to heaven, but where were his wings? All these people beside and behind Grandma and Anna Grace started filing by the shiny gray box. Most everyone was crying and wailing as they passed by. Then Mama screamed a terrible yell, "Pa, Pa. Why did you die?"

At that moment Anna Grace remembered what Daddy had said, "All of us want to go to that place called heaven." Why in this world was everyone so sad? Anna Grace was waiting to see Grandpa get his wings and fly to heaven. At that moment the short, fat, droopy-eyed Mr. Grouch closed the top of the shiny gray box, and somehow Anna Grace missed seeing Grandpa get his wings and fly to heaven. With the shiny gray box closed, Mr. Grouch led everyone back to the car, with Anna Grace leading the way.

Back at the house everyone was eating, drinking, and talking about Grandpa. The old biddy with the big nose and straight black hair pulled into a knot kept saying he was a fine man. "He would give you the shirt off his back," she said. If only she knew what Grandpa called her: Miss Busybody Biddy.

Anna Grace was so confused. Everyone was saying over and over such good things about Grandpa. Mama was always saying he was going to corrupt Daddy. Anna Grace didn't think he could corrupt Daddy because he loved that hot dog and beer just like Grandpa.

All of his buddies from Chick's Café were at the house eating fried chicken and barbecue and drinking sweet ice tea, but Anna Grace thought they wished for the hot dogs and cold beer at Chick's Café with Daddy and Grandpa shooting the bull and listening to Gene Autry sing "Home on the Range."

# School-Sickness-School

After Labor Day in Anna Grace's sixth year, she started school, leaving behind Ellie Mae, Billy Bob, and Lilly Lee to play with each other. Every morning Grandma would walk the three blocks to school, holding Anna Grace's hand tight. The two of them were almost inseparable after Grandpa died. Singing all the way to school, holding her lunch bag of a peanut butter and jelly sandwich plus a big red apple, Anna Grace started her grandma's day in a happy mood. Every morning Grandma gave her a nickel for milk, but Anna Grace could not drink the milk because it constipated her. Sometimes the constipation was so bad, she would bleed. Mama said for her to drink water. Instead of giving the nickel back to Grandma, she saved it; then she would drink from the water fountain. At the water fountain she put her foot on the pedal, then reaching as high as she could, Anna Grace would put her mouth on the spout to drink the cold water. Anna Grace knew the Depression had been hard. It left the family with the desire to save everywhere and everything, so Anna Grace saved her nickel every day.

## Seven, No More

After the Christmas holidays, Anna Grace began feeling tired and sleepy and throwing up everything she ate. Her face, arms, and legs looked very yellow; the whites of her eyes were yellow. She carried a slight temperature, but she continued to go to school.

Mama said she just wanted to stay home and play, because Ellie Mae and Billy Bob were playing with her toys while she was away at school, but that was not the reason. Anna Grace was tired and sleepy. At school the kids would not play with her because she looked funny. When she wore her yellow dress, her face would look yellow too. Why couldn't Mama see that she was sick? Before Grandma walked her to school, Mama would burst out with a yell to Anna Grace, "Go to school, you lazy, spoiled brat. You will never amount to anything."

After two weeks of crying and crying every day, Mama and Daddy had a big fight about Anna Grace, whether or not she was sick. Daddy said, "We will take her to see Dr. Jones. He will know if she is sick."

Off they went to Dr. Jones, Daddy and Mama with Anna Grace lying in the back seat of Miss Susie, which was the name for the family car, while Grandma stayed home with the other children.

Dr. Jones looked into Anna Grace's eyes, ears, and throat, hitting her knees with a rubber hammer. All of a sudden Dr. Jones stopped. Her reflexes were not good, and her complexion was very yellow. He told them Anna Grace was very sick and contagious. Anna Grace had bacteria hepatitis: very contagious bacteria, which she probably got at school drinking out of the water fountain. Anna Grace was the second person from school to get sick. Dr. Jones said, "Take Anna Grace home, isolate her from everyone, keep her comfortable, giving her this medicine," handing Mama a bottle of medicine. Dr. Jones said, "I will be by tomorrow to see her."

With Anna Grace feeling tired and sleepy, Daddy lifted her into his arms, carrying her to the car. On the way home, Anna Grace slept in the back seat while Daddy drove Miss Susie. Mama and Daddy didn't speak to each other on the way home.

With the curtains open in the bedroom, Daddy lifted Anna Grace into the bed. All alone, Anna Grace knew what "contagious" meant now. No one else could be around her except Mama and Grandma. Both of them were very careful about washing their hands; they didn't want the bacteria to spread in the family. Anna Grace was used to sleeping with Ellie Mae and Grandma, but now this big bed was hers alone. After a long nap Mama came into the room with medicine and tomato soup. With a spoonful of that awful medicine sliding down her throat, Anna Grace just gagged. She didn't want to throw up because she would have to take it again. Anna Grace thought the medicine made her sleepy. After eating the soup, she fell asleep again. There were many days of taking medicine, eating soup, and sleeping. Even though Mama and Grandma came into the room to care for and comfort her, she felt so tired and alone. It's bad for a six-year-old to be confined in a room with no one to play or talk with. Every day, even on Sunday, Dr. Jones came by to check her.

At first on his visits, his eyes were sad with no smile on his face. Talking with Mama, Daddy, and Grandma, Dr. Jones said that he "would do everything in his power for Anna Grace," but he suggested that the family pray for her recovery. "She has a long time ahead to recover, if she makes it."

When Anna Grace was not sleeping, she was watching Ellie Mae and the children play outside. Anna Grace felt so

## Seven, No More

alone, even though Mama said Jesus was in the room with her all the time. Anna Grace never saw Jesus, but she was sure he was there. Every time the door opened, Daddy would blow kisses, saying he loved her. Anna Grace missed being with everyone, but she did not want her family sick.

Spring was coming. The crocus was blooming in beautiful bright colors, and the buttercups were the most beautiful shade of yellow and white that she had seen. The grass started turning from the brown straw of winter into different shades of green. Anna Grace was getting better. Her fatigue was going away, and she could walk around inside the room without being exhausted. Anna Grace was eating better also; she was consuming food other than soup. Her complexion was slowly returning to normal. Still very sick, she tired easily and stayed sleepy. Could the fatigue be caused by the medication? Every night Anna Grace wanted to know when she could go outside. It had been about four months since she was outside. Mama told her Dr. Jones would let her know how soon she could go outside. Dr. Jones was coming by twice a week. He sounded pleased that Anna Grace was doing well.

In order to encourage and comfort her, Grandma would play bird cards with Anna Grace. She really got good at bird cards; she won almost every time. She could name almost all the birds in the batch of cards. Anna Grace and Grandma had long talks together about her future. Often Grandma asked what she wanted to be when she grew up. Some days she wanted to be a nurse or a teacher, and other days she wanted to be a mama, but most of all she wanted to be a grandma just like her. First, though, she had to get well.

In late spring Anna Grace started getting stronger. Dr. Jones was coming once a week, and he was thrilled with her improvement. Dr. Jones said, "You can go outside to bathe in the sun; but you can not play with the children just yet."

It was great to get some sunshine and fresh air, and to see the outside of her room. One thing that Dr. Jones was concerned about was her fatigue. Everyone in the neighborhood and the town was so concerned about whether or not Anna Grace would get well. In her heart she knew she would get well because Jesus stayed in her room giving her strength, easing her loneliness, and creating a desire to get well. There were so many things in her life that Anna Grace wanted to do. Many times she wondered how Mama and Daddy paid Dr. Jones, because she knew he must have charged a lot to come to see her so often.

One day Anna Grace asked Grandma how they paid Dr. Jones. Grandma just shook her head with tears in her eyes and said, "This world is full of wonderful people, and just don't you worry about it."

All the time Anna Grace was sick and isolated, her hair grew long. Mama started braiding it into long pigtails. She looked very different with braids and ribbons. It was a good thing to look different. Anna Grace was starting to be healthy again.

In late summer of her seventh year Anna Grace was feeling good enough to play outside again. The bacteria that made her sick were gone. School time was approaching; the girls were excited they would be in school together. Grandma was busy getting the flour sacks clean and ready while Mama was busy sewing for the girls. Anna Grace and Ellie Mae needed new dresses for school.

During the last eight months everyone in the family was busy helping Anna Grace recover. Now the time had come for her to return to school; everyone was helping with making it a pleasant experience. Daddy took her and Ellie Mae

*Seven, No More*

shopping for school supplies since both of them were going to first grade.

Because Anna Grace missed most of the first grade, she had to repeat it. From that day, her peers thought she was not as smart as them, especially having a younger sister in the same grade. Ellie Mae was just five and Anna Grace was seven years old. Little did they know that everything Ellie Mae knew, Anna Grace had taught her. Her sickness and confinement made stronger than ever her desire to succeed. Although she wanted to make friends with her classmates, there was one boy she especially wanted as a friend. He probably thought she was dumb because she was seven years old and in the first grade. Wearing a pink printed dress with pink bows on her long braided hair, Anna Grace would not wear a yellow dress since she had been sick, leaving all the yellow dresses for Ellie Mae to wear with her red hair. Anna Grace pranced over to sit in front of that cute boy. My gracious! That put Anna Grace on the front row. About that time Anna Grace decided to show him and the rest of the class how smart she was. *Maybe being on the front row would show everyone who is the smartest,* Anna Grace thought, *especially that cute boy.* His name was Roger; Anna Grace liked him the first time she saw him. He must have liked her too, because he tied her pigtails into a knot.

On the playground Anna Grace chased him in tag, and he chased Anna Grace in tag. That's the way first-graders do when they are in love. Roger told her he would be her boyfriend if she gave him her nickel every day. Anna Grace let him know that he was crazy if he thought she would give him her nickel. She didn't need a boyfriend if she had to buy him.

# War on the Horizon

The Great Depression was getting better. More people were getting jobs with enough money to buy food and the necessities for their families, but on the horizon a war was raging in Europe. Adolf Hitler set his goals on capturing all of Europe and creating a perfect race of people. With Japan and Italy as his companion countries, he was sure he could accomplish his goals. His fascism controlled the young men of Germany, while the older men were interested in the wealth and power victory would bring them. Anna Grace would hear the grown-ups talking among themselves about how evil Hitler was, how America would be in war against him soon. Many grown-ups were concerned about their sons going to a foreign land and fighting a war. Aunt Barb's husband and Uncle Clem were already in the United States Army. Quite possibly the two of them would be among the first to go to war.

Daddy said the Great Depression was bad. The family had survived that terrible time, but was the United States prepared as a country to handle the hardships of another world war? On December 7, 1941, in an unexpected attack,

## Seven, No More

Japan bombed the United States base in Pearl Harbor. Many soldiers died. President Roosevelt declared war on Japan, and the country was in grief and turmoil. Families with loved ones in the service of the country were praying for their safety. Mama, Daddy, and Grandma prayed for the safety of Uncle Clem and Aunt Barb's husband along with all the other soldiers. The United States Army started drafting young men into service. For those men who didn't pass the physical or were specially trained in a vital field of service, the government put them in nonmilitary service.

One day Daddy came home from work to find a notice in the mail for him to report to Fort Bragg for examination for the United States military draft. The United States needed him to fight for his country. Mama started crying. The next two days were sad at the house; then on the third day Daddy went to Fort Bragg. After his examination, he came home happy; the United States government needed him to help build ships in the Newport News shipyard. With his welding skills, he was going to be building ships for the government. His job of building ships was just as important as carrying a gun fighting the enemy. The United States government needed ships to transport soldiers, supplies, and equipment.

The family was very proud of his contribution to the war, and with pride in their hearts they sent him to Newport News. His work schedule included a twelve-hour shift, twelve days straight with two days off for rest. Daddy was used to long hours and hard work, but not being away from his family. Nearly every other weekend Daddy came home to see his family; that was more than the soldiers could do. Some of them would never see their family again. On the two days off, Daddy would hitchhike home if he didn't have the money to catch a bus.

# Our Trip to Newport News

Occasionally Mama would take Ellie Mae, Billy Bob, and Anna Grace on a bus trip to Newport News for a visit with Daddy. Lilly Lee stayed with Grandma; she was still a baby. Managing three children on the bus was hectic, especially with Billy Bob on board. On one such occasion the family was boarding the bus filled with soldiers and their families heading to their assigned post when Billy Bob—who was four years old—shouted out loud, "Look at those Japs. We need to get them."

Many of the soldiers heard him, but one of them in the back of the bus said, "Okay, buddy, we will get them."

Mama was so embarrassed that she grabbed Billy Bob and told him to be quiet. Billy Bob had a way of getting attention solely on himself.

All four of them huddled together eating peanut butter crackers. Mama had some sweet tea in a colored jug from which everyone took a drink, washing down the peanut butter crackers with the ice tea. The trip was really long, as the bus stopped at every bus station in all the little towns. At the

## Seven, No More

Roanoke Rapids bus station, the bus driver stopped for a toilet visit and food. Roanoke Rapids was another cotton mill town with a bus station like the family had back home. There were many mill towns up and down the bus route.

Anna Grace was glad the driver remembered that people needed to use the toilet. For two hours the family had been drinking and eating; the driver must have heard Anna Grace say she had to pee right now. If he hadn't stopped the bus, he would have some stuff to clean up. Billy Bob held his stuff as long as he could. Peeing in his pants was not uncommon for him.

After going to the bathroom, they looked around the bus station. Some soldiers and their families were sitting on round stools, eating hot dogs, and drinking colas and beer, just like at Chick's Café. All those years Anna Grace had thought Chick's Café was different from every other eating place, but she was wrong. Every town had a place like Chick's Café.

Anna Grace told Mama, "If Daddy were here, we could have a hot dog and a drink."

A soldier who overheard her approached Mama, offering to buy the kids a hot dog and a drink. Mama said no thanks.

Mama was really a proud woman. She couldn't stand for people to think the family was poor, and they weren't poor. They just didn't have any money.

After a little while, the bus trip continued. Everyone was excited about seeing Newport News, and of course seeing Daddy too. The arrival at the bus station was timed with Daddy's finishing work for the weekend.

The five of them gathered their luggage along with the

*Marlene Rose*

peanut butter crackers and tea and walked to the rooming house where Daddy stayed.

Upon arriving at the rooming house, the rest of the family met Mrs. Fuller, who owned the house and took care of all the roomies. She greeted Mama and the kids and told Daddy to bring his family downstairs for supper. The children thought they'd be eating peanut butter and crackers all weekend; little did they know what a good meal they would have! Mrs. Fuller had some good food—some meat with potatoes, green string beans, buttermilk biscuits with honey and butter, and apple pie with ice cream. *No wonder Daddy stays here, with all that good food,* the kids thought. Mrs. Fuller told Mama that the children made her think of her grandchildren. Mrs. Fuller was a tall, slim lady with blond curly hair and big blue eyes; she didn't look old like the children's grandma. When the war broke out, Mrs. Fuller decided to open her home for boarders because these working men at the shipyard needed somewhere away from home to call home. Her husband worked at the post office; all their children were grown and married. She had a big house with six bedrooms and the biggest kitchen the family had ever seen. The table was shaped like a horseshoe with twelve chairs. The stove covered one half of the room, with cabinets on either side. With the help of her housekeeper named Shelly, the two of them prepared all the meals and kept the house clean.

Shelly was a beautiful black girl around twenty years old. Her husband was drafted into the military and was serving in North Africa. Over three months had passed without her hearing from him; she was worried about his safety. Mrs. Fuller kept Shelly busy with cleaning and cooking; Shelly made all the desserts. Her favorite was apple pie, which she made from scratch. In the morning when Shelly swept the porches and walkways, she would hesitate and look into the sky, questioning the whereabouts of her husband. Even though her heart was broken, she kept a smile on her face and bounce in her feet.

At the rooming house the family all slept in the same room. With Shelly's help, Mrs. Fuller brought quilts for them to sleep on the floor. Shelly and Mrs. Fuller were wonderful and made everyone feel right at home.

After the visit with Daddy, they returned home on the late Sunday evening bus. All four were huddled together in the double seat: Mama holding a sleeping Billy Bob, Ellie Mae and Anna Grace holding on to each other to stay awake.

It had been a long but joyful weekend. The children thought it was wonderful to see Mama smiling again. She was always ill-natured and grouchy, but not tonight. It was nothing for her to bite the kids' heads off for even thinking about mischief, but not tonight. Tonight, she was very different. She had a smile on her face and was constantly humming, very softly. Daddy must have made her happy on this weekend trip, or she just needed some time away from the mill town, Grandma, family, and everyday, mundane life. Whatever, she was certainly a changed woman—so confident, content, and happy. The trip home did not seem to take as long, even with all the stops the bus made, maybe because Ellie Mae, Billy Bob, and Anna Grace took catnaps. While Billy Bob slept, Mama held him, looking out the window, but she couldn't have seen anything because the night was so dark. Maybe she was daydreaming at night, or she could have been thinking about Daddy, how much she missed him, or

*Marlene Rose*

maybe she was thinking about Lilly Lee. Upon arriving at their home bus station the family scrambled out holding hands, with Billy Bob hanging on to Mama because he was still sleepy. They walked the four blocks home in the dark. No streetlights were burning in this small town, but the children were not afraid. They had each other.

Grandma was so excited to see everyone coming home. Everyone, except maybe Mama, was thrilled to be home. All at once she seemed sad again. While the family was away, Grandma missed having them around the house making a mess for her to clean, but she enjoyed having Lilly Lee with her.

After Grandpa died, Daddy insisted Grandma come live with them, even though she was Mama's mother. Daddy loved her so much and did not want her to be alone. At first he had to convince Mama how much Grandma could help with the children—especially Anna Grace, who was always into mischief. When Anna Grace was sick, Grandma was a real blessing to her and the family. A lot of time and care was needed in caring for Anna Grace, and Grandma helped with her. Anna Grace adored Grandma, and the feeling was mutual. Maybe Mama thought Grandma spent too much time with her. Often Mama would say under her breath, "There are other children in this family."

Many times Grandma would reply, "It's your turn with Anna Grace; I will help with Ellie Mae, Billy Bob, and Lilly Lee."

When Daddy was home for the weekend, Grandma cooked everything he liked. Daddy would praise her for cooking, cleaning, and caring for his family. At times Mama must have felt left out of the family. In her own way she shielded herself from everyone around her. She must have thought Daddy was the only one who loved her.

With Daddy working in the shipyard and Grandma helping with the children, Mama continued to work at the mill. She said the family needed the money to make ends meet, when really Mama needed the job for her personal satisfaction. The only time Mama didn't work at the mill was when she was having another baby.

# Rationing and Air Raids

Sometime after World War II was declared, everything started being scarce again—not that it was ever plentiful. In most families or maybe the families Anna Grace knew, both parents were working unless the husband was drafted into service. Many fathers were drafted into nonmilitary service, leaving a void in the family that many grandparents filled. Grandmothers often took care of the children while the mothers worked, providing parental care that kept families together. Nearly everyone was affected by the war in one way or another. Uncle Clem and Aunt Barb's husband were serving in Eastern Europe. Anna Grace heard Grandma say many times that "God would bring our soldiers home safe because our country was a God-fearing country. We are fighting Satan. It will be great when this war is over. How much more can our country endure?" First the Depression, and now the war.

Certain foods were scarce, because the military needed the sugar, oils, and basic foods to feed the soldiers. Every

## Seven, No More

essential product the military needed was made available. To the general public, these products were rationed. On May 5, 1942, rationing began, with a sugar book containing twenty-eight stamps; later, coffee, butter, and oils were included. Then in February 1943, canned goods, frozen foods, and red meat were rationed through books of stamps. It didn't matter a great deal to the family that food supplies, gas, and rubber products were rationed because money was scarce at home anyway. One thing for sure: Daddy was getting what he needed, because the military needed the shipyard workers. The military needed ships, tanks, and barges for defense; therefore, the government made sure these nonmilitary workers were cared for.

Of course, people of great wealth were able to get what they needed and wanted through the black market. Grandma used to say, "If you have enough money, you can buy your way anywhere, except heaven."

Mama and Grandma learned to cook without the rationed commodities, and their 1937 Ford named Miss Susie got some needed rest. Occasionally Daddy would get enough gas to drive the Ford to Newport News for his twelve working days and then back home again. Most times Daddy would ride the bus or hitchhike home to save money. All the extra money he saved was advancing their cause of freedom from debt.

One Saturday when Daddy was home from the shipyard, he decided to have the kitchen chairs caned. Daddy had saved a few dollars from his cigarette money. Working at the shipyard twelve hours straight, he didn't smoke as much as he did before the war. From his buddies at the mill, he heard about Tom, a black man from the east side of town. These buddies said Tom was by far the best and cheapest weaver of

## Marlene Rose

cane in the whole world. Good and cheap made Daddy happy, so off to the east side of town Daddy went to look for him. When Daddy returned home, Tom was with him. Into the kitchen the two of them went for the chairs. These chairs had stacked newspapers in the seat. Sometimes Daddy's backside would slide through the bottom of the chair. That notwithstanding, these chairs needed more than newspapers in the seat to hold a person Daddy's size. At the boarding house all week, Daddy had chairs with bottoms that held him while he ate. As Tom started caning the first chair, the town siren went off. Immediately all the lights went out; not even a cigarette or candle could be lit. The whites of each other's eyes were all they could see shining bright. Tom was so afraid. Ellie Mae and Anna Grace were afraid too, but not Billy Bob. The girls ran to Daddy for safety. *What was going on?* Daddy explained that enemy planes could spot even the tiniest flicker of light if they were flying in the skies. All lights had to be out so the town would not be a target. The sirens continued for a long time, making the darkness frightening. Everyone was quiet except Tom. He dropped to his knees calling on the Lord for mercy. "Save us! Save us!" he was shouting above the sounds of the sirens. Surely these airplanes were going to fly by. Was it too late to ask God for mercy with the planes in the air above them? Maybe not! No planes bombed the town that night, because all the target lights were out . . . or maybe because the Lord was answering Tom's prayer. They never knew.

Later that night Daddy told one of the reasons they may have been targeted: their nearness to several military bases. Another reason for the sirens could have been to see how prepared they were for such a disaster as a secret attack. At any time the planes could have bombed them: they had lit-

## Seven, No More

tle defense against them. It was a long time before the town had lights again. Daddy walked Tom home, because Tom was terrified. The chairs were never caned; the newspapers continued to mount in them. Daddy still had his cigarette money. The caning of the chairs was the least of their concerns. Many times in the middle of the night, the sirens would go off for the townspeople to take cover. The roaring of the airplanes would wake Anna Grace and her family. Sometimes it sounded like the skies were full and her little body would just tremble with fear and anxiety, not knowing if they were going to be bombed by the Japanese or Germans or if it was a friendly patrol drill. Thanks goodness they never had to experience the awful bombings. It was a sad and dark time in the history of the United States. Daddy remained at the shipyard, building carriers for the government, coming home every other weekend.

Along about early spring Mama started getting fat again. Grandma asked, "When are you to be delivered?"

Mama replied, "Late July or early August." Maybe Daddy would be home for the delivery and help with the children.

Spring was filled with sugar and cooking oil rations. By now, a lot of goods were rationed. Sirens were going off almost every night, causing blackouts. Grandma made sure everyone was fed; the children were ready for bed before the darkness of the night crept upon them. Daddy was still working at the shipyard, coming home every other weekend, hoping the delivery would be one of those weekends. Every day Mama and Grandma gathered all the vegetables from the small victory garden that the two of them planted in the spring. Every night they would snap beans, shell peas, and clean corn while Ellie Mae, Billy Bob, and Anna Grace played unless the sirens went off. After a siren, there was no

*Marlene Rose*

more work or play. All the lights would go out, and huddled together in one of the beds in the bedroom would be Ellie Mae, Billy Bob, Lilly Lee, and Mama. Anna Grace and Grandma would be snug in the other bed. They never knew if it was a real attack or a drill. They just took cover in case of a real attack, scared stiff, not able to speak. Anna Grace could imagine bombs falling from the sky, lighting up the town with massive fires. After the sirens, it was a long time before they could talk again. It was an unpredictable time with the war in Europe, threatening the United States as well. Billy Bob was always asking if the enemy were coming to bomb them. He wanted to fight them. After the sirens stopped and the lights were shining again, they felt an eerie calmness. Not knowing if another siren would go off that night that might be a real attack, they were very afraid and had trouble going to sleep.

Mama suggested the children close their eyes and count sheep in the darkness. In the darkness they could not see any sheep. After such a frightening experience, they all needed a good night's sleep. Anna Grace would hold on to Grandma's hand all night. The next morning, Grandma would get busy again. With Mama working the first shift at the mill, Grandma took control of the house and the children. After they were fed and dressed to play, Grandma needed help to get the chores out of the way.

While Grandma boiled water in a big navy blue container called a canner, Ellie Mae and Anna Grace did the dishes. Grandma put the string beans in glass quart jars filled with water and a teaspoon of salt in each jar. After sealing the lid, she put the jars in a rack inside the canner that was filled with hot boiling water. The beans boiled in that water for an hour, but it seemed like all day. Steam filled the kitchen.

## Seven, No More

During the winter these beans were a treat, served with winter vegetables from the garden. The winter garden consisted of sweet potatoes, collards, turnips, and pumpkins—the best food in the world, along with buttermilk biscuits made with mayonnaise or butter that Mrs. Collins brought them. Even though Mrs. Collins missed Daddy and his work with them, she did not forget the family, bringing them milk, eggs, and butter. With wonderful people like the Collinses, the family was well fed. Daddy could hardly wait to come home for Mama's good cooking.

Outside Ellie Mae, Billy Bob, and Anna Grace played with two little girls next door. Kate and Jane were Ellie Mae and Anna Grace's ages. They all had a good time playing together until Billy Bob decided he wanted to play cowboys and Indians. Billy Bob would chase them, pretending to shoot with a stick he found in the yard. Billy Bob tried to scare the girls. Both Kate and Jane were afraid of him, but not Ellie Mae and Anna Grace. They knew how to cope with him. Always the sheriff, Billy Bob wanted Anna Grace to be the Indian because she was the darkest in the crowd. How did he know what an Indian looked like? The only Indian Billy Bob saw was in the comic books belonging to Pete. Lone Ranger and Tonto were Pete's favorites. Always looking at comic books, Billy Bob lived in a dream world. Sometimes dreams were not so bad, because they allowed a person to forget the realities of everyday living. Oftentimes the children played make-believe house. In the yard they piled dead fallen branches into rooms; they imagined a much finer house than their own house. Billy Bob was always Daddy, setting on a stump pretending it was a chair and smoking a cigarette. Always Daddy had to be on good behavior. Billy Bob was taking lessons.

# The Outhouse

Oftentimes when Pete and Sally came to the house to play, Granny would be wearing her navy canvas walking shoes and dressed in a light blue denim dress going below her knees and her short black curly hair pinned behind her ears. She would walk with them, even though Pete was nine years old and Sally a year younger. With the war going on, Granny tried to keep her family nearby or else know where they were. During one of those visits, Mama agreed for Ellie Mae, Billy Bob, and Anna Grace to go home with Granny, Pete, and Sally for supper and to play. With Mama's excess weight and hot summer weather, she was in no condition to argue with the children.

As soon as they arrived at Granny's house, Anna Grace had to pee. Granny didn't have a toilet on the back porch; instead she had an outhouse. Anna Grace was scared stiff to go into that house. Pete told them about the awful creatures in there: spiders, snakes, flies, and rats. "Don't be afraid," Granny said. "I will show you how to pee, and the critters will not bother you."

## Seven, No More

So Granny and Anna Grace went into the outhouse. With her eyes wide open, Anna Grace looked all around but did not see any of the creatures that Pete was always talking about. Leaving the door open so they could exit fast, Granny stood up on the bench over the hole with her legs spread, holding up her dress and peeing.

That looked easy enough, so Anna Grace jumped up on the bench, spread her legs over the hole, and started peeing though her panties. She started to cry. "Mama will get me. How come you didn't pee on your panties, Granny?" she asks.

Granny replied that she never wore panties. She wanted to always be prepared, whatever that meant. The two of them were so fast going into the outhouse and peeing that the creatures didn't have time to wake up. After everyone peed, they returned to the house to wash their hands. Granny brought a blue basin filled with cold water, plus a half-melted bar of soap for washing. Anna Grace felt like she needed to wash something else too, but she didn't.

While Pete, Sally, Ellie Mae, Billy Bob, and Anna Grace played, Granny cooked supper. Mama said Granny could take nothing much and cook the best meal in the world. Anna Grace remembered the wonderful blackberry and pecan pies she kept in that cabinet that Granny called a pie safe. Pete told them she kept them there for safekeeping from little brats. Pete always had a smart mouth. Billy Bob liked being around him. After supper and before Granny returned the children home, Daddy came by with Lilly Lee. Granny asked him, "What is wrong, son?"

Daddy replied, "She's getting ready to deliver tonight, and Aunt Barb has gone to visit her new in-laws. I need some help."

*Marlene Rose*

Granny told him the children would be fine at her house tonight. Anna Grace looked at Daddy as if to say, "I can't stay," but she didn't. She was still thinking about the outhouse and the critters.

As if she read Anna Grace's mind, Granny assured her that she didn't have to use the outhouse at night. "We have a potty chamber that we use at night. In the morning we will empty the potty into the hole in the outhouse," she said.

Anna Grace thought that might be all right, knowing in the morning she would be going home to her own toilet. Pete was not afraid, so he could empty the potty. Next on her mind, Anna Grace wondered where she and Ellie Mae were going to sleep.

The tiny house had only two bedrooms, and each bedroom had only one bed. In Anna Grace's house, there were two beds in every bedroom, which made six beds. Because they didn't have enough people in the family to fill all the beds, Mama was always inviting someone to stay. Friends and family were always welcome. Many times they would accept her invitation and stay for a while, and some stayed as long as a month.

The plan was for Granny and Sally to sleep in one bedroom while Pete slept in the other bedroom, because Granny thought Pete would never give up his bed. Anna Grace and Ellie Mae were content to sleep on the floor in Granny's room.

Much to Granny's surprise, Pete said, "The girls can have my bed, and I will sleep on the floor with Billy Bob."

Ellie Mae and Anna Grace should have known he was thinking about mischief. Off to bed they went, with Lilly Lee sleeping with Granny and Sally.

In the middle of the night, Ellie Mae screamed.

## Seven, No More

Everybody came running. "Something was crawling on my legs," cried Ellie Mae.

Then Pete replied, "You imagined that. You're afraid of your own shadow, Ellie Mae. Look at Anna Grace. She is not afraid. Right, Anna Grace?"

Anna Grace shook her head, even though she was not as brave as Pete said she was. The girls laid back down, trying to go to sleep. All at once they heard this scratching noise. "It's a rat. Let's get out of here," she said. Taking Ellie Mae by the hand, scared stiff, the girls ran to Granny's room.

"Let us sleep on the floor," Ellie Mae cried. "Let Billy Bob sleep in the bed with Pete. Both of them are fearless."

Before breakfast the next morning, Daddy arrived at Granny's with a big smile across his face. By that look, everyone knew there was another Billy Boy in the family.

Much to their surprise, though, the family had a new little girl. "Let's go see her," everyone cried at once. After the night Anna Grace and Ellie Mae experienced, they wanted Billy Bob to stay with Pete and Granny, but that didn't happen. They all went to see the new baby girl. On the way home Daddy said their new little sister was beautiful and tiny, but Mama was not doing well. With instructions for all the children to be as quiet as possible, they hurried home.

Mama was still in bed, with Grandma sitting beside her and holding the baby. "What are we going to name her?" asked Grandma.

Mama looked at Anna Grace and said, "You name her."

"Holly Rose," Anna Grace replied without hesitating. "Let's name her Holly for the beautiful holly tree with red berries at Christmas and Rose for the beautiful red roses of summer."

## Marlene Rose

Being pleased with the choice of the name, Mama told Daddy that sounded good to her. "Holly Rose she is!"

The birth of Holly Rose took much toil on Mama. She was always tired and ill-mannered. In a flash, she would bite your head off. Grandma said it was mostly because of the stress of taking care of the children and the home, and working at the mill besides. With Daddy gone so much, she felt the pressure to do it all. Maybe it was because she had so many children; now there were five.

Now things would be better because at least the war was coming to an end, On May 9, 1945, the president made the speech on national radio that the war was over. Gas would flow again, and the rationing of food would soon cease. Maybe it was time for Daddy to come home. Mama needed him!

# Return to the Mill

In early winter, Daddy returned home from the shipyard to begin life again in his old job. His buddies at the mill were thrilled, but not nearly as much as Mama and the children. Grandma was glad too. While Daddy was working at the shipyard, Mr. Farris started courting Grandma. Although Grandma seemed happy with Mr. Farris, Mama thought she was rushing into the relationship. Grandpa had only been dead for four years, and Mr. Farris had lost his wife to cancer just two years before he met Grandma. She had been sick for a very long time, and he had not been in a hurry to find another wife until he met Grandma. Of all the places to meet someone, it happened at the grocery store that Mr. Farris owned. Mr. Farris moved to their town four years before Grandma met him. Because of his wife's illness not many people in town knew him. The two of them bonded immediately. They had many of the same interests, and each of them had grandchildren and family serving in the war.

Finally Grandma told Mama that she and Mr. Farris were

getting married. After the wedding, she'd be moving into his house. Mama and Daddy gave their blessings. The wedding took place at the First Freewill Baptist Church, with Grandma looking beautiful in her gray-blue dress and hat with the pearl earrings and necklace that Mr. Farris gave her as a wedding gift. Mr. Farris wore a black suit and was showing off his gray curly hair. He was a handsome man, and Grandma was a lovely lady. They made a handsome couple. Mama dressed in her best dress and Daddy arrived in his Sunday suit; they stood up for Grandma and Mr. Farris at the wedding, welcoming Mr. Farris into the family. All the children were sad that Grandma was moving from their house, but they were thrilled that she was happy. Grandma assured them she would visit often. The children seemed happy to hear that, especially Anna Grace.

With Grandma leaving for her new home, Daddy returning home from the shipyard, five children and now another baby on the way, Mama decided it was time for her to stop working at the mill. Besides cleaning and caring for the children, she found time to cook three meals each day.

In early summer after school was out, Mama thought Daddy needed a good hot meal and sweet tea for supper. After all, that was the least she could do for him since he was working the second shift. Their neighbor was working the same shift with Daddy. He had a boy and girl about the same age as Ellie Mae and Anna Grace. Their names were Meg and Sam. The two sets of parents decided the four children could take supper early every evening to the mill for their daddies.

So one early afternoon, the four of them started to the mill with supper for each daddy. Mama had fixed Daddy country-style steak with potatoes and gravy, lima beans, and biscuits in a tin bucket with the lid on tight. She filled a half-

## Seven, No More

gallon jar with sweet tea and ice. Sam and Meg's mother fixed fried chicken, corn bread, and string beans in a black metal lunch box with a handle. His sweet tea was in a tall black thermos.

About halfway to the mill, the children stopped to rest. It was so hot, the sweat was pouring down their faces. Anna Grace and Ellie Mae had sweaty hair, even though they had pigtails. Meg had short bobbed hair that looked like she had been playing in the water, but Sam—with his hair cut short—was soaked to the scalp. They were a mess. Sam suggested they take a swallow of the cold ice tea. Everyone agreed that the daddies wouldn't miss four swallows. So Ellie Mae and Anna Grace took a drink from Daddy's jar. Both of them worked to loosen the lid, but finally they had to let Sam do it. Sam and Meg drank from the black thermos. That ice tea was delicious, and even with the heat there was still ice inside. Off they went. Another block passed. They stopped and took another swallow of ice tea. Off they went again swinging the tin pail and black lunchbox. After they had gone about seven blocks, stopping along the way to take a drink, they stopped and looked to see how much ice tea was left: just enough tea for one more round to drink. At that time, they also decided to look at the supper they were carrying: it was intact. Everything looked the same: mush everywhere.

After crossing the railroad tracks, still swinging the supper pails, something grabbed Anna Grace's pail, pulling the lid off. Mush went everywhere. To make matters worse, Sam tried to help by putting half of what he was carrying in Daddy's pail. He wanted to share, but as he did, he dropped the metal box he was carrying. It became mush also. To the children's amazement, Sam looked up and said, "What are we going to tell them about the ice tea?" Ellie Mae replied, "Tell the truth. We drank it."

Daddy was not mad about the supper. He knew they were just children and were thirsty, but from that day forward he carried his supper. Daddy understood being a child meant doing crazy things. He was just glad he was home to experience all those wonderful things.

With Daddy home and being able to buy gas, the family traveled to the nearby big city once a month to buy food staples. It was much cheaper than buying at the local market even though Mr. Farris owned the market. All five children would ride in the back seat of the black '37 Ford; there was not enough room for everyone to sit on the back seat. Anna Grace found herself sitting on the hump between the seats. It seemed every time they rode in the car, Anna Grace was destined to sit on the hump. Feeling like the stepchild, Anna Grace said, "It's someone else's turn to ride on the hump. Maybe Billy Bob should take a turn."

Fuming and fussing, Billy Bob pointed to Ellie Mae, saying, "When did you last ride on the hump?"

Ellie Mae, feeling a little out of sorts, shouted back, "I have been on that hump as much as I plan to be. Lilly Lee, get on that hump now."

Fearing Ellie Mae, Lilly Lee sat on the hump. She thought to herself, *Coming back is your turn, Ellie Mae,* but Anna Grace was on the hump again. Being the oldest child, Anna Grace was supposed to look after her siblings.

Once while they were on their way to the grocery store, she asked her daddy to please stop the car. He wanted to know why. She said, "Throw some of these young'uns out." Mama replied, "Maybe you should be first." Daddy didn't stop. Maybe Mama didn't understand that everyone was

## Seven, No More

breathing down each other's throat. Anna Grace could hardly wait till she was old enough to stay home by herself. Sometimes Anna Grace felt like a stepchild. She could never do or say the right thing to please Mama. She missed Grandma!

After arriving at the grocery store, everyone went inside to shop. Running here and there in the grocery store, all the children were helping fill the cart with their favorites. Ellie Mae put oranges, apples, and bananas in, while Billy Bob put in cookies shaped like fish. Anna Grace tried to slide some chocolate candy in the cart, but Mama caught her, saying, "Put it back. You don't need it."

They filled the grocery cart so fast it would make your head swim. Daddy was doing his best to keep the five children in tow. Hurriedly Mama shopped, looking at her list, hoping she didn't forget anything. She forgot to get washing powders; she didn't want to scrub those clothes with lye soap. The kids made sure she got their favorite cereal. After checking the groceries and paying for them, they carted the load out to the car. Into the back floorboard the grocery boy put the bags. With Anna Grace sitting on the hump, she thought, *What a mistake that was.* He didn't know these children. Daddy started the car and down the road they went toward home, which was a good thirty-minute drive. All five made sure Mama bought the right cereal. By the time they got home, most of the cereal was gone—right into their stomachs!

# Moving

With five children and another baby on the way, the family needed a bigger house. In early fall after church one Sunday, Daddy took them for a ride in the black 1937 Ford, Miss Susie. Riding in the country, they passed many beautiful fields of orange pumpkins peeping out from under the withering vines. All of a sudden, Daddy stopped: a house and ten acres of land for rent. Both Mama and Daddy looked at each other, and sparks flew! The next thing Anna Grace knew, they were moving into that house.

What would they do with ten acres? That was good for a big playground; well, maybe not if Mama kept having babies. But Daddy had a plan for his family to reach the freedom he dreamed for his children. At dinner on Sunday he shared his plan: plant eight acres of cotton and the balance in vegetables, supplying the family with food and money from the cotton. In addition to working at the mill on the second shift, he would use his mornings to clear the land for spring planting.

## Seven, No More

The loan of a mule and plow from one of the neighbors, Mr. Weathers, made the breaking of the land much easier for Daddy. The mule's name was Maude. Every time Daddy went to the field with Maude, Billy Bob followed him.

"Wanting to ride that red mule that looked like Tonto's horse," Billy Bob said.

Mr. Weathers's kindness on loaning different farm tools made the whole family's chores much easier, Daddy acknowledged. Mr. Weathers was a thin, drooped-shouldered, slight man with a snarl on his face all the time. Living in the home place and never marrying, he seemed quite content. He was friendly and helpful with Daddy, but he let the kids know right away he didn't want any children coming into his yard and messing with his dog and cat. He didn't want any children around, period. Never did Anna Grace see a smile on his face, and his piercing blue eyes behind glasses looked right through her. He probably could tell when children were mischievous. Anna Grace didn't want to mess with his old ugly black dog, but she would have liked to have held that blue-eyed black cat. Never did she get brave enough to hold the cat, though, because Mr. Weathers always had an eye on her. Little Holly Rose didn't even notice Mr. Weathers; she toddled over to the cat, Lucy, picked her up, and carried the ten-pound cat around like a sack of candy. Holly Rose was only twenty-three pounds herself! What a feat and joy for her to carry that blue-eyed black cat around.

With a stick in his hand, Billy Bob liked to chase Mr. Weathers's black dog. Mr. Weathers would get so mad with Billy Bob that his blue eyes turned green. Anyway, Mr. Weathers liked Daddy and all he was doing to provide for his wife and children. Often Mr. Weathers would tell Mama, "You have a good man." Mama agreed! She knew Daddy wanted a better life for his family, and he was willing to work to find it. Sometimes Mama invited Mr. Weathers over to eat on Sundays. The five children would just stare at him eating. You could tell he was alone all the time, because he ate without talking to anyone. At dinner or suppertime, it was the family's time to share their day, so they talked a lot!

After lunchtime, Daddy would go to his job at the mill. Now that they lived two miles out in the country from the mill, Mama prepared Daddy's supper for him to take with him. She made sure he had plenty of sweet ice tea. He thought the distance was too far for the children to walk with his supper, and without Sam and Meg around, going to the mill wasn't fun for them anymore. In the early spring, very early in the morning, Daddy would harness Maude and plow the rows for planting the cotton.

On Saturdays, everyone would help with the plantings. The children would make a hole with a stick, drop a cottonseed in the hole, and cover the hole with dirt, making a pat with a foot. Sometimes Anna Grace put several seeds into the hole before covering it. She was ready to get rid of those seeds before they planted the eight acres. After planting cotton came the garden. In early February they planted slips from the potatoes; then in late May they were ready to harvest. While waiting for the cotton and vegetables to grow, they harvested the potatoes. Mama fixed potatoes at least ten different ways.

Daddy would plow down the middle of each row, throwing the potatoes out of the ground, and then the children would dig around in the dirt to find them. A game they played was to see who could fill their baskets first. Ellie Mae always won. She would use her hands and feet to dig in the dirt to find the potatoes to fill her basket. Billy Bob would

*Seven, No More*

cry because he never won the game. How could you win a game if you stopped playing before it was over?

In the spring when the cotton and vegetables started growing, each child would help hoe the weeds and grass away. By the time the vegetables were ready to be harvested, the children had golden suntans that the rich people in town would have died for. With suntan lotion on their arms and legs, the young people from town would lay in the sun until they burned or blistered. All Anna Grace and Ellie Mae had to do was work in the field, wearing shorts and T-shirts.

As part of Daddy's plan, all the money from the vegetables that were sold at the market would be divided among Ellie Mae, Billy Bob, and Anna Grace. His only request was that they save at least 10 percent of the earnings: he was starting the kids on a plan to be free. Being twelve years old going on thirteen, Anna Grace wanted to buy new clothes like her peers at school, and to buy school supplies like pencils, scissors, paints, and colored papers for all her artwork. Many of the pictures she cut from the Sears Roebuck catalog. She used them in her artwork, but she still needed the art supplies. At that time in her life she wanted to be a designer when she grew up. Before Anna Grace spent any of her money, she gave her tithes to her church. She listened to Daddy, and she remembered what her late grandpa said: don't forget to put a little money away for tomorrow.

And Grandma used to say, "Don't ever forget God, he is always with you!"

After picking the cotton, they took it to the market to sell. They made twelve bales on eight acres of land. What a crop! Because they used fertilizers and insecticides early in the growing season, Daddy was able to pay for them because he paid the house and land rent at the end of harvest time.

Daddy, Mama, and the children did all the work, leaving a good profit from raising the cotton. Off to the bank Daddy went to open a savings account for his family. They were on their way to freedom and a new life. God was good to us!

# Anna Grace Faces Death

All summer long the weather was almost unbearable. Polio was spreading among children and adults. The family had one tragedy after another. Uncle Clem developed an alcohol problem that Mama swore was caused by terrible memories of the war. Aunt Barb's only daughter was diagnosed with the terrible disease of polio. She was in the hospital for a long time. Mr. Weathers fell and severely injured his head, and it looked like he would never be normal again, whatever that is. And then Anna Grace started feeling sick.

For three days and nights she vomited until the vomit was clear as water, all the time carrying a temperature of 103 degrees that would not be broken. Wearing a thin pink cotton nightgown, she lay in the bed too sick to sit up. One minute she was freezing with blankets thrown over her; the next minute she was hot and thirsty. To satisfy the thirst, she drank some cola, but that cola would come right back. Because she was so weak from vomiting and the high temperature, oftentimes she would miss the pail when vomiting

*Marlene Rose*

and would throw up on the bed. Mama was always changing the sheets and pillowslips, then washing them in hot water to kill the germs. Mama remembered the bout with bacteria hepatitis. Could this be a reoccurrence? Keeping cold, wet washcloths on her head because it hurt so much, Anna Grace kept her brown eyes closed. She was a sick girl. Mama thought maybe she had a virus or an upset stomach from something she ate. Wasn't polio supposed to be caused by a virus? If the upset stomach was from something she ate, why was no one else sick? Could it be that the insecticide was not completely washed off the vegetables? Mama thought maybe her system was just not right at that time.

On the third day, both Mama and Daddy looked worried. Daddy said, "Let's take her to see Dr. Jones."

With Daddy carrying Anna Grace to the car, because she was too weak to sit up or stand, they went as fast as Miss Susie could take them to Dr. Jones's office. Her complexion had taken on a gray look, and her brown eyes had a cloudy and dull expression when she opened them. Most of the time her brown eyes were closed and her lips were red from the temperature. With a frown on his face and somewhat puzzled, Dr. Jones asked, "How long has she been sick?"

Mama replied, "About three days and nights. Every day she seemed to get worse." Mama was sure it had to be something she ate, because she had not been around anyone sick.

With some reservation, Dr. Jones told them to watch for any changes in the stiffening of her limbs or neck. "With polio raging, we cannot be too careful." When Dr. Jones finished with Anna Grace, Daddy carried her to the car with Mama following close behind them, very quiet. Not a word was spoken on the way home. Upon arriving home Daddy carried Anna Grace into the house, putting a light blanket

## Seven, No More

over her chilled body. Anna Grace fell asleep with cold wet cloths on her head. *Why didn't Dr. Jones give her some medicine to stop the headache?* Mama wondered. Mama asked everyone to be a little quieter and let Anna Grace rest. All the children spoke in whispers and played quietly.

During the night Anna Grace woke Daddy crying. He had been asleep in a chair beside her bed. Mama had been staying with her every night and day, and she was exhausted. "My stomach is coming apart," Anna Grace cried. Naturally Daddy thought she had to vomit, so he grabbed the chamber. Most of the vomit went on the bed and Anna Grace. He tried to clean her as much as he could. Everything that came up was green and smelled terrible.

Immediately he called out to Mama: "We are going to the hospital." Daddy told her to call Mr. Weathers to stay with the children.

While Mama was calling Mr. Weathers, Daddy wrapped Anna Grace into some warm blankets, gathered her in his arms, and carried her to the car, making her as comfortable as he could while waiting for Mr. Weathers to come care for the other children. Daddy started the car. "Sure am glad we have enough gas," he said. Mr. Weathers arrived half-asleep, but not for long with these children. Both Mama and Daddy left for the hospital with Anna Grace asleep in the back seat.

At the hospital, the admitting nurse asked them, "What doctor sent you?"

Daddy explained to her about their visit to Dr. Jones's office that morning. Dr. Jones told them to watch her for any changes—stiffness of the limbs and temperature rising—but she was getting worse even without those exact symptoms. When the nurse looked at Anna Grace, she knew this girl was very sick. She called for the emergency room doctor.

*Marlene Rose*

After looking at Anna Grace, he ordered blood tests, X-rays, and cardiograms at once. He told the nurse, "This situation is very serious. Let's get everything done now."

The doctors and nurses kept coming into the emergency room and taking her temperature, which by now was 104 degrees. "We have to stabilize her before we can take any more tests," the doctors said. As the nurses were bathing Anna Grace in an alcohol solution, the emergency room doctor ran back into the room. "The blood test shows she has a ruptured appendix. A surgeon has been called. We can't wait any longer to do surgery. With all that poison running in her body, her life is in danger." While the surgeon was on his way to the hospital, Mama and Daddy were called into the admitting room to sign some papers for Anna Grace to have surgery.

"Urgent" was the word everyone was using. The surgeon talked to Anna Grace's parents, telling them what he was going to do in surgery. "We will remove her appendix, what is left of it, and clean out all the poison surrounding it. The situation with your daughter is very serious. We will do everything we can to save her life. The surgery will last about two hours, then recovery at least another two hours. So get some rest, and we will let you know something as soon as possible."

Off to the waiting room the two of them went, holding on to each other. Mama was in her wrinkled print housedress with her hair tied in a ponytail with one of the girl's ribbons. On her feet were the bedroom shoes she wore every morning. They must have been beside the bed when Daddy woke her. Dressed in jeans and a white T-shirt with his black curly hair matted together, Daddy looked a mess. He had probably slept in those clothes and forgot to comb his hair

*Seven, No More*

before they left home. The two of them never left home looking this way, but this was an emergency.

After waiting about two hours, Grandma and Mr. Farris arrived. Fear was all over Grandma's face, while she and Mr. Farris hugged Mama and Daddy. Preacher Jim showed up about the same time. Word had gotten around town that Anna Grace was in the hospital having surgery.

Preacher Jim began to tell them, "Hold on to your faith. God knows where you are. He will deliver Anna Grace from this terrible time."

Everyone in the waiting room knew her chances of recovery were not good. The poison from the ruptured appendix was spreading like wildfire. About two hours after Anna Grace went into surgery, the surgeon came into the waiting room. Looking grim, he told them, "The surgery went well, but Anna Grace is a very sick girl. We will know more when she wakes up. She will be in the recovery room another two hours. When she is transported to her room, Mama and Daddy can stay with her, but no other visitors today! In a couple of days we'll see about visitors." The doctor must have known all of the big family would visit together. Several times the doctor inserted in his conversation, "Rest, rest, rest for Anna Grace." Feeling better about Anna Grace, Grandma and Mr. Farris went home to care for the other children, and to free Mr. Weathers.

By the time the two of them arrived at Anna Grace's house, Mr. Weathers was exhausted from running after Billy Bob, Ellie Mae, Lilly Lee, and Holly Rose. Big Black Dog and Lucy missed their food, so they went looking for Mr. Weathers. What a mistake that was! Dragging Lucy around like she was a bag of candy was little Holly Rose. Poor Mr. Weathers was trying to stop Billy Bob from hitting the Big

Black Dog with a stick. After gathering his cat and dog, Mr. Weathers went home without asking about Anna Grace. Grandma thought that was a little strange, but Mr. Weathers was unusual.

After a day and a night passed, Anna Grace started stirring in her bed. Both Mama and Daddy had been by her bedside, and they were thrilled to see the movement. Mama was getting fleshy again, so it was hard for her to reach over the bed but she managed. Giving Anna Grace a spoon of ice, she asked, "How do you feel?" Because it hurt to talk with all the tubes in her nose and mouth, Anna Grace just stared at them and shook her head "okay." Green liquid was coming out of her body into one tube, and liquid fluid with penicillin was running into her body from another tube. For another a day or two Anna Grace continued to feel better. Then all of a sudden in the middle of the night, her temperature jumped to 104 degrees and her incision burst, with green and yellow pus oozing out. The infection was like a thick syrupy mass, slowly running from the incision. Around the incision was a hard mass, which meant more infection.

The redheaded, blue-eyed nurse called for the doctor on duty. Looking at the incision and the massive infection still inside, he called the surgeon on duty, who happened to be the original surgeon.

The doctor on duty told the surgeon, "If we don't operate immediately, this girl is going to die."

Nurses and doctors were scurrying around the room, getting her ready for emergency surgery. Her life was in danger.

After the second surgery, Anna Grace stayed in the recovery room for a very long time. The doctors had to make sure she was awake before they took her to her room. Mama and Daddy were sick with worry. Each of them was blaming the

## Seven, No More

other for not realizing how sick she was. Late morning Anna Grace was brought back to her room. According to Mama, Anna Grace looked very gray and pale, almost lifeless. She was worried that Anna Grace was still very critical. Without any warning, Anna Grace slipped into unconsciousness. Her temperature was 104 degrees, yet she was freezing. One of the nurses said she had gone into shock.

"With cold packs on her head and warm blankets on her body; she will be fine in a little while," said the redheaded, blue-eyed nurse on duty, wrapping Anna Grace in warm blankets. That "little while" lasted three days and nights.

While Anna Grace was unconscious, a big bright light appeared unto her. Her spirit left her body and went to the big bright light hovering over her body. She could see the doctors and nurses in their white uniforms with masks over their mouths, wearing rubber gloves and working continuously over her, trying to save her life. Tubes and more tubes of medicine were being pumped into her body, while other tubes were draining the thick green poison from her. Her temperature remained the same at 104 degrees, yet her body was cold as ice, even with warm blankets covering her. All around the bed, the doctors and nurses were talking quietly, trying everything they knew to do. No response! As one team of doctors and nurses left, filled with fatigue and anxiety, another team of staff members would take over caring for the sick girl. Everyone was exhausted, including Mama and Daddy standing at the foot of her bed, crying and praying for her life. It looked like nothing would work. Anna Grace was aware of everyone and what they were doing to save her life, but her spirit was in another space out of her body. Anna Grace could see them from her position above the pale lifeless body, but her spirit couldn't decide to return to her own body. The big bright light hovered above the body, and her spirit stayed with the light.

Standing at the foot of the bed between Mama and Daddy was Preacher Jim, holding their hands. Preacher Jim started to pray, and as he began to pray the hovering light started moving toward the body. The big bright light guided the spirit of Anna Grace back into the body.

With great wonder, she opened her eyes and smiled. Tears of joy filled the room. Anna Grace was on her way to recovery. Along with Mama and Daddy, Preacher Jim and the staff at the hospital were all very thankful. Many times in the hospital room, Anna Grace looked around trying to find the bright light, but never did. Anna Grace even asked Mama and Daddy, "Did you see the big bright light?" They said no.

In her mind, Anna Grace decided God was not ready for her yet!

After seventeen days in the hospital and two operations, Anna Grace returned home to recuperate. Looking pale and feeling exhausted, she stayed in bed resting a lot. Lying beside her was Angel, her long-haired gray and black Persian cat. She was a gift from Grandma and Mr. Farris. Mr. Farris had several cats when Grandma married him, and she learned to love them. Angel was from one of Mr. Farris's cats' litter. She was beautiful with long, shaded gray/black hair and blue eyes that smiled unless she closed them while she was purring. She was about six months old and so loving. She often lay on Anna Grace's bed cuddled up to her.

Mr. Farris said, "She knows how sick you are. She is helping you feel love and security by cuddling close to you."

Mr. Farris must have been right, because each day Anna Grace was feeling better. Her bland diet of bread, soups, and liquids was getting boring. Mama started putting a little more substance into her daily diet. Every day she sat at the table for all three meals, even though her food was different from the rest of the family.

Sometimes Ellie Mae would blurt out, "Why does she eat that way? Why can't she eat like the rest of us? She has always been the pet around here."

Daddy tried to console Ellie Mae by saying, "Anna Grace had two operations on her stomach, so her stomach needs time to recover. Plus, heavy foods she cannot digest yet. She is still very weak. Why don't you be a little more understanding?"

Mama, seeing how jealous Ellie Mae appeared, said, "Ellie Mae, if you were sick like Anna Grace, we would treat you the same way. She is no more the pet than you or any other child in the family."

Ellie Mae sounded off with, "Why does she get to keep that Angel cat on her bed, Mama? You don't even like cats."

Mama replied, "If that cat helps her to get well, she can keep her. Mr. Farris and Grandma were wonderful to bring her Angel. Our main concern now in the family is to help Anna Grace get well. She faced death, but she returned to us."

Billy Bob just listened to everyone talking, then he asked, "Why can't Harvey stay in the house? He will not pee on the floor; he is trained. We wouldn't have a litter box for him like we do for Angel."

Daddy understood and answered him, "Harvey is our guard dog. He barks to alert us to visitors or trouble. Do you remember when the snake was crawling in the yard? Harvey warned us, thank goodness! None of the little ones were bitten by the snake because Harvey protected them. We need him outside."

While the family was having dinner, they were talking about their different concerns about Anna Grace and her health. Anna Grace asked if she could return to bed. She was tired and sleepy. Leaving the table, she told Mama, "Thank you for a good meal, and thank you for taking care of me." She left the table.

Returning to bed, she cuddled Angel in her arms and went to sleep. When Anna Grace woke up, Holly Rose was asleep beside her, also cuddled up to Angel.

With Anna Grace getting better, everyone could see how much Angel helped her in her recovery by giving her unconditional love. Angel became the pet in the family, with everyone brushing, feeding, and loving her. Even Billy Bob would fuss for his time with Angel.

With all the friends from the mill village and church coming to visit, Mama stayed busy. She was getting fleshy again, and the time was drawing near for her to deliver.

Preacher Jim came by a couple of times each week, praying for Anna Grace and the family. Before leaving, he always had a glass of Mama's sweet ice tea.

One night after the younger children had gone to bed, Anna Grace was still awake and heard Mama tell Daddy, "God had something special for Anna Grace by letting her come back to us." Never once did Anna Grace hear them refer to the big bright light when she was unconscious, but Anna Grace thought about it a lot.

# Going to Church

The family became real involved with church following Anna Grace's hospital stay because of her life-threatening illness. They went every Wednesday night and two times on Sunday. The family was thankful to have Anna Grace back in good health again.

The church was in a former storefront building on the east side of town near the mill village where Daddy worked. They started going to that church when they still lived in the mill village. All of the members were so concerned about the family during the crisis with Anna Grace's illness and showed much love. Preacher Jim came to the hospital every day to visit and pray. Mama said he reached Jesus for Anna Grace when she was unconscious. Both she and Daddy said they would forever be grateful to him and the church for their kindness.

The church's sanctuary housed about forty painted wooden benches with a raised platform in front of the pews. On the platform was the Bible stand for Preacher Jim. In

*Marlene Rose*

front of the Bible stand was an altar rail and communion table with silver-colored cups for the wine and a silver-colored tray for the bread, all resting on a white starched tablecloth.

For warmth in winter, the church had a potbelly stove that used black coal. During the winter, each male member took turns building the fire, filling the stove with coal to keep the fire burning. Sometimes the building got so hot that people began getting sleepy, but with the fiery preaching of Preacher Jim and the anointed singing, everyone stayed awake—well, mostly everyone. Now, summertime was completely different: no potbelly stove!

All that was necessary in the hot sizzling summer was to open the windows and doors, letting both the breeze and bugs inside. With funeral home picture fans, people shooed the bugs away and moved the breeze a little. With long-winded fiery preaching like Preacher Jim's. sometimes Daddy's friend Mr. Johnson would fall asleep with his mouth wide open. That mouth was a perfect bug catcher.

Outside the back of the church was a separate building with a toilet for the church members. The building was far enough away from the main building that the odor stayed outside the church, especially in the summertime.

Before each service, Daddy took the children to the toilet. Calling each one by name, he asked, "Do you need to pee?" Patiently Daddy waited while everyone used the toilet.

Going first was Anna Grace, taking Holly Rose with her; next came Ellie Mae with Lilly Lee, prompting her to hurry, "There are people outside waiting to use the toilet," she said.

Last Billy Bob went alone into the toilet. He didn't stay long, but he used most of the toilet paper. After Billy Bob

## Seven, No More

left, Daddy checked to see if everything was intact inside. Usually most of the paper was gone.

After the toilet visit, the family marched into the church like ducks in a row following their mama. Mama would lead the way, wearing a big floating navy dress with a white pilgrim collar. The children thought that she was trying to hide her being fleshy again.

Next came Lilly Lee, dressed in a pink print dress with ruffles around the hemline. She had a big pink bow in her short dark hair, and she wore black patent shoes with pearl buttons that Anna Grace outgrew. Following her was Holly Rose with that matted curly hair. She would wear a red and white polka-dot dress, and carrying her little bag to match. Mama made that dress and bag just for her. Holly Rose loved bags, bags, and more bags. Anna Grace followed Holly Rose, wearing a white sleeveless dress that showed her beautiful dark suntan. Next Ellie Mae was trying to push in line. She didn't want to sit beside Billy Bob. He always got her in trouble by talking to her. Her yellow voile dress, collarless with butterfly sleeves, set off her blazing red hair tied up into little curls. Knowing Ellie Mae didn't want to sit beside him, Billy Bob got behind her, punching her as they marched into church. As she turned around, he stuck out his tongue. Billy Bob was wearing his navy pants and white shirt with a little red bow tie. He looked like he would be a good fill-in for Preacher Jim. Sitting next to Daddy, Billy Bob had to behave, so Ellie Mae thought. She didn't count on him behaving though, because he didn't know how. After Daddy sat down, he crossed his legs. No getting up. If anyone needed the toilet, they had to wait!

As everyone stood to sing the opening song, the children grabbed the songbooks. Ellie Mae and Billy Bob would share, and Billy Bob started poking her in the side. With Daddy singing, he didn't notice the two of them until Ellie Mae punched Billy Bob so hard, he fell against Daddy. Mama saw the commotion. She nodded for Ellie Mae to move away. It was Lilly Lee's time to sit beside the troublemaker, so Ellie Mae traded places with Lilly Lee. That put Ellie Mae beside Mama. Lilly Lee moved next to Daddy, leaving Billy Bob in between Holly Rose and Lilly Lee. All around him were girls. How could he win?

After the singing and praying, Preacher Jim read the Bible. As he preached, all the children listened except Billy Bob. He was fast asleep!

# Sara Beth

After the harvesting and selling the cotton and vegetables, it was time for Mama to deliver again. Just about everyone hoped for another girl, except maybe Mama. For some reason, she thought that boys were so special. Could she not remember how Billy Bob always peed on everything? Billy Bob bullied the girls every chance he had. With Aunt Barb having moved away, Grandma married to Mr. Farris, and Mr. Weathers, their neighbor, being a little old and senile, the only person left to care for the children was Granny. As time was drawing near for the delivery, Daddy had to get things settled. Anna Grace was almost thirteen years old. She could take care of the smaller children, but Mama said no. She didn't want her to experience taking care of four children at home while Mama was in delivery. The children needed to leave home for Mama to have the baby. "Maybe if we have enough money the next time she has a baby, she can go to the hospital," Daddy said, "like Anna Grace when she was sick."

## Marlene Rose

Off to Granny's house Daddy went, to ask if she would care for the children while Mama was in delivery. Caring for the five children was a big deal, but Granny agreed! Ellie Mae and Anna Grace could help with Lilly Lee and Holly Rose, but not that Billy Bob. He and Pete could do some damage if they were left alone.

Before Daddy went to see Granny, he talked to Billy Bob, promising to take him fishing at the Neuse River if he behaved. What a deal! If there was anything Billy Bob liked better than fishing, it was more fishing. He loved going to the Neuse River for fishing and looking at the wildlife. Billy Bob agreed he would be good and not let Pete get him into trouble.

The very next morning, Mama started having pains. She told Daddy, "Take the children to Granny's house." By now, after having five children, she knew what to expect and what to do in preparation for a new baby.

Because they lived two miles from town out in the country, Daddy was afraid to leave Mama alone. "We need to find someone to stay with you. Let me get Mr. Weathers to stay until I return," Daddy said to Mama.

"No way," Mama replied. "It will scare him to death. You know we need him with the farming next spring."

Loading up the five children with Billy Bob sitting in the front seat and the rest of them in the back, Daddy drove Miss Susie to Granny's house. Billy Bob thought that because he was a boy, he should ride in the front seat with Daddy. The girls knew what he wanted: to talk about fishing. Fishing was the main subject he talked about, after cowboys and Indians.

Off to town Daddy went, stopping by Dr. Jones's office to tell him that Mama was ready to deliver. "Who's with her?" Dr. Jones asked.

## Seven, No More

"No one," Daddy replied. "I'm taking the children to their granny's, and I will be right back. She assured me she would be fine for that length of time."

Dr. Jones didn't like what he heard. Hurriedly he told his nurse that he had to deliver a baby. The people waiting could come back this afternoon or in the morning. He had an emergency! Down the road he went to deliver the next baby in the family.

Daddy and all five children arrived at Granny's house all excited. As Daddy left them, he reminded Billy Bob about his promise. The girls just stared at Billy Bob, because they knew he didn't know how to be good for five minutes, let alone two hours. Billy Bob promised, and Daddy believed him.

After Daddy left for home, Billy Bob conversed with Pete. Ellie Mae said, "Those two are up to no good."

Anna Grace thought she may be right. "Let's wait and see. We will be ready for them," she said.

The two boys were discussing fishing. Billy Bob said, "Daddy is going to take me fishing after that baby comes. Maybe he will take you too, since you are his baby brother."

"All right," shouted Pete. "I love to go fishing at the Neuse River, but I am not a baby brother, understand, Billy Bob?"

Daddy had one fishing pole and line but he could rig something for Billy Bob to use. Pete was lucky. He had his own fishing pole and line because he went fishing with Granny all the time. It must have been nice to miss school when you wanted to go fishing. Pete did that more often than he should. There's one thing for sure: Daddy would not let Billy Bob do that. So Billy Bob and Pete were going to be good and not bully the girls. Both of them knew Ellie Mae and Anna Grace could take care of them.

On the way home from Granny's house about a mile from his house, the car ran out of gas. Jumping from the car and running the distance home as fast as he could, Daddy got there before Mama delivered. Mama had done all the things that Grandma used to do, so she was ready when Dr. Jones arrived. Mama was experienced in having babies. She was much calmer than when she delivered Anna Grace. With Anna Grace being her first baby, she was scared to death.

In less than two hours Daddy carried gas to the car, then went to pick up the children. Much to their surprise Daddy told them they had a new baby sister. Her name was Sara Beth, because she had beautiful red hair like Mama's Aunt Beth. The girls were thrilled to have another red-haired sister like Ellie Mae. Ellie Mae jumped with joy, because now she could have company in the family. Sara Beth could share some of the teasing about their red hair when she got a little older.

# Fishing

When Sara Beth was about ten days old, Mama was feeling better, even though she had worked in the cotton patch and the garden before her delivery. Sara Beth's delivery was not nearly as bad as Holly Rose's. Grandma said the stress of Daddy being gone, all the children, and working at the mill made her delivery so hard when Holly Rose was born. Every day now, Mama was doing a little more. Ellie Mae and Anna Grace were a big help with the other children, especially Lilly Lee and Holly Rose.

Billy Bob was still harassing Daddy about going fishing, so Mama had heard as much about fishing as she wanted. "Take that boy fishing," she said, "before he drives me crazy."

So Daddy told him, "We will go fishing next Saturday." Overjoyed, Billy Bob started getting his fishing supplies together. First his hat, to keep the sun out of his eyes; his clothes—long pants and long-sleeved shirt—to keep the sun from blistering him; his glove, to take the fish off the hooks; and an old clean rag, to use when handling the fish. He did not have a fishing pole, but he was not worried because Daddy promised to make him one.

The girls heard that Daddy and Billy Bob were going fishing; they wanted to go, but Daddy told Lilly Lee and Holly Rose that they were too small. "A big fish might gobble them thinking they were bait," he said.

The two little ones started crying, so Mama promised they could help with Sara Beth. That was all the two of them wanted to hear. They were going to "play mama" with that baby. Ellie Mae and Anna Grace were going fishing. Ellie Mae knew she would catch the biggest fish, but what were they going to fish with? Billy Bob told them not to worry; Daddy would make them a fishing pole just like the one Daddy was going to make him.

Daddy had each child go in the yard and find a stick as long as they were when they stood up next to it. It needed to be an inch in diameter. Then they should bring the stick to him. He put a nylon string near the base, tying it on the end and leaving the string as long as the stick. Last, at the end of the string, he tied a lead weight, cork, and hook. "Put the bait on the hook," Daddy said, "and you are ready for the fish to eat. Coming this Saturday, we will arise at 5:00 A.M., because that's when the fish eat breakfast. Since we have poles and lines ready, we will need to stop at the Rock Store for bait. All good fishermen go to the Rock Store for bait. They have big, fat, juicy worms, crickets, and shrimp." Billy Bob liked those juicy worms for fishing. "Everyone will need to get a cold drink and nabs to take for lunch. Fishermen don't eat packaged lunches."

Billy Bob told Daddy, "Those girls don't know how to fish. They will never put a worm on their hooks."

Daddy replied, "Then we will bait the line for them."

## Seven, No More

"Gee whiz," said Billy Bob. "I thought this was going to be a man's outing. I asked Pete to join us."

Daddy replied, "That's fine. We will ask Granny to come and fish with the girls."

All at once things seemed to be getting better. Pete and Granny had fishing poles, and Granny knew how to fish. Billy Bob wanted to throw back the fish that he caught, but Daddy said, "Granny will cook them. We will eat the fish we catch."

Ellie Mae and Anna Grace were thrilled that Granny was going fishing with them. She might be able to give them some pointers on how to catch fish.

It was about 6:00 A.M. when they got to the Neuse River. Out of the car the group jumped, gathering fishing poles, worms, crickets, and shrimp. The boys went one way and the girls another, all looking for the perfect fishing hole. The best place to fish was in a thicket of bushes with a clear path to the water. As Ellie Mae and Anna Grace were walking behind Granny, talking about who was going to catch the biggest fish, they heard the bushes rattle.

Anna Grace knew Pete and Billy Bob were trying to scare them. "We will not let them scare us," said Ellie Mae.

About that time the girls saw Granny swishing a stick—one, two, three times into the bushes. "I got him. He won't bother anybody else," she said. "Come on, girls, we have to find our fishing spot."

Before they followed Granny, they looked at each other and decided to look in the bushes to see what Granny was talking about. Then they saw it: the biggest, longest black snake they had ever seen.

The girls didn't walk to Granny; they flew, and said, "No snake is going to get us if we see him first."

*Marlene Rose*

"He's dead," Granny said. "I beat him to death with my fishing pole. Now come along, girls, and stay with Granny." She didn't have to invite them twice.

While the girls were finding their way, Pete, Billy Bob, and Daddy were catching fish. "I caught a big one," Pete hollered. "I think he is a brim."

Billy Bob screamed in excitement, "I got a big one. A big catfish. I bet Granny doesn't want him to cook, though. He eats all the stuff in the water," said Billy Bob, sounding disappointed. But she did.

At the end of the day, with their catch of brim, catfish, carp, and bass, they started walking down the side of the riverbank to go home. Everyone caught something except Ellie Mae. She was trying to untangle her fishing line that was caught in a tree and watching for snakes.

Just about the time Ellie Mae got untangled, Billy Bob made the smart remark, "We would starve to death if we depended on her and Anna Grace."

Ellie Mae heard him, and she started chasing Billy Bob along the side of the riverbank. The banks were slippery and muddy from all the recent rains. As he was looking back to see how close Ellie Mae was, he slipped on the mud and slid right into the river—feet first. Running close behind, Ellie Mae hit the same spot and slid right into the river behind him.

Granny yelled to Pete, "See if you can get those young'uns out of the river." Into the water Pete jumped, and the three of them started splashing each other. Something started swimming toward them. Billy Bob, Pete, and Ellie Mae started swimming to the bank as fast as they could. The water behind them kept moving, and as they climbed on the

*Seven, No More*

riverbank, they saw a big green snapping turtle swimming toward them.

"He must weigh at least ten pounds," Pete said with excitement in his voice. "Let's catch him. Granny will make us turtle soup." Just at that moment, as if the turtle heard him, he swam away.

"Oh, heck," said Pete. "I don't like turtle soup anyway. I was just kidding. Let someone else catch him."

# Driving Miss Susie

Living out in the country, Daddy used the car to drive to work most days. With a neighbor who also worked at the mill on the second shift, they decided to carpool. Even though the distance was only two miles, it helped to share expenses and to have someone to talk with on the way home late at night.

Dressed in blue denim jeans, a red/green plaid shirt with big, heavy brown combat boots—he got used to wearing these boots while working at the shipyard—and holding a cigarette between his lips out of the corner of his mouth, Daddy would go off to work.

Their car was named Miss Susie. She was a beautiful, shiny black car with four doors and a hump in the floorboard in front of the back seat. Miss Susie had four on the floor and big, beautiful headlights with shiny metal rings around them. She was a fast Ford. Daddy was a Ford man, and he liked fast black cars. On Saturday afternoons Daddy would fix a pail of soapy water and wash Miss Susie and her big beautiful headlights, rubbing the metal rings till they shined like new coins. Miss Susie had to be cleaned for Sundays. After church and dinner, Daddy would drive Miss Susie into the big city with his family. He would dream about living there some day.

When Daddy washed the car, Lilly Lee was always with him in the yard. She would wash and polish the headlights. Lilly Lee loved those shiny big headlights, and every time she found a clean rag she was polishing those headlights.

When asked why, Lilly Lee would simply reply, "Miss Susie likes to have her lights clean when we go to church at night, so she can see well. It is my job to keep them clean and shining because Daddy drives her to and from work."

One Wednesday afternoon, Mama and the children were bored stiff staying home. It was a hot and miserable day; not even the birds were moving. Harvey, their dog, was lying in a freshly dug hole under the oak tree near the back porch. Miss Susie had been at home for a couple of days, so perhaps she was bored too. She may have been missing her friends in the parking lot at the mill. So Mama decided Miss Susie and the family needed a ride. Calling all the children together, she informed them, "We are taking Miss Susie for a drive."

To begin with, Mama didn't know where the starter or the ignition was. She had seen Daddy do some juggling with gears in the floor, so that made her an expert on changing gears. The only thing she knew was the steering wheel, because it stared right in her face. Wearing a big red and blue print housedress—because she was getting fleshy again, or maybe because she had not lost all the baby fat from Sara Beth—and navy blue canvas shoes, she gathered all the children into the car.

Ellie Mae sat in the front seat with Mama, and the rest of them climbed into the back, with Anna Grace holding Sara

*Marlene Rose*

Beth. It was so hot that even with all four windows down and a slight breeze blowing across inside the car, they could hardly breathe. Lilly Lee and Holly Rose had sweat running down their faces, and Billy Bob was swearing about the heat. "It's too darn hot for even a fish to swim."

Putting the keys in the ignition, Mama turned the starter on Miss Susie. She didn't make any noise. Mama tried again, and Miss Susie still didn't make any noise.

Finally Lilly Lee, with her five years of wisdom, said, "Maybe I need to clean Miss Susie's headlights: she likes for them to be clean."

Mama didn't want to drive Miss Susie with dirty headlights, so she let Lilly Lee clean them. Lilly Lee got a clean rag out of the rag box on the back porch and started cleaning the headlights. After cleaning and shining the lights, she piled back inside the car between Billy Bob and Holly Rose, both of whom were sweating and beginning to argue. Lilly Lee was the only one to keep them straight, with Anna Grace holding Sara Beth and Ellie Mae in the front seat beside Mama. After Lilly Lee got back in the car, Mama tried to start the car again, and this time it worked. Maybe Lilly Lee knew what Miss Susie wanted: clean headlights.

Slowly Mama started out of the driveway. All of a sudden. out of her window Ellie Mae saw a car coming about a half mile down the road. "Stop, stop," she cried, and Mama slammed on the brakes. At least she knew where the brakes were.

Ellie Mae hit the dashboard hard enough that she thought she broke her head. "Maybe you can't drive," she said. "Did you ever get a driver's license?"

Mama said, "Be quiet, Ellie Mae. I don't need a license to drive Miss Susie. I will just take her for a drive down those

## Seven, No More

back roads. We won't meet anyone there, especially a patrolman." Maybe Mama didn't know that patrolmen go down back-country roads, or she was just taking a chance. Out on the highway they all went, with Miss Susie bumping and grinding. Mama thought she knew how to change gears. Back and forth she pulled that gear stick the way she had seen Daddy do. Miss Susie jumped and bumped. Poor Miss Susie didn't want Mama driving her. She was Daddy's car.

Still sitting in the front seat with a knot on her head as big as a hen's egg and her face pale as cotton, Ellie Mae said, "Mama, she doesn't want you to drive her. We had better take her home."

Without any warning, Mama steered to the right. Miss Susie went into the ditch on her right side with her left-side tires up in the air spinning and with her engine still running. Mama turned off the engine after Billy Bob told her the car might blow up with the gas running out upside down.

With all the windows down, they were lucky they didn't go flying out the window or just fall out of Miss Susie with her landing on top of them. One by one they climbed out of the windows, with Ellie Mae climbing over Mama, who was lodged under the steering wheel. Anna Grace handed her Sara Beth, then Lilly Lee and Holly Rose. Billy Bob knew he could get out by himself, but his clothes hung up on the door handle. He pulled his shirt loose by tearing it apart to free himself. Then he slid down the door, leaving a two-inch scratch in the middle of the door. Mama was trapped between the steering wheel and her big stomach. Finally Anna Grace was able to free her, and the two of them climbed out the window.

With her hands on her hips, looking at smoking, smelly tires, Ellie Mae said, "Oh, Lord, Daddy will get us!"

# Jim Boy!

With Sara Beth approaching her second birthday, Mama was getting ready to deliver again. Everyone hoped she had that second boy she wanted so much. The house was already full of girls, with Anna Grace, Ellie Mae, Lilly Lee, Holly Rose, and baby Sara Beth. This time Daddy told the children he had enough money for Mama to go to the hospital for her delivery.

Ellie Mae asked, "Why does she want to go to the hospital? All of us were born at home. We are fine, except maybe Billy Bob. She probably knows she's having a boy. Gee whiz, we'll have another Billy Bob."

Anna Grace replied, "Maybe this is extra special for Mama. She said this is her last baby. She seems to think she's too old to keep having babies. Why, one of Mr. Weathers's neighbors just had a baby. Mr. Weathers said she is at least thirty-five years old, and Mama is only thirty-four years old. She could have at least one more baby, couldn't she, Daddy?"

"Well," Daddy replied, "I suppose she could, but that lady

# Seven, No More

only had two children. This will make Mama having seven. That is the big factor in Mama not having any more babies."

"Well, if this baby is not a boy, I bet she will try again," said Ellie Mae. "Why does she want another boy so much? Billy Bob doesn't help with the dishes or clean the house. The only thing he does is talk fishing and destroy everything he touches."

Grandma said, "Mama wanted another boy so she could have her own preacher man in the family."

"You know, Grandma," said Ellie Mae, "if she lets Billy Bob train him, he probably will be a policeman, fireman, soldier, or cowboy. Billy Bob is fascinated with anyone wearing a uniform, especially if they are carrying a gun."

"Maybe Mama will let Ellie Mae and Anna Grace teach him," said Lilly Lee.

"We could teach him to be a singing preacher," Ellie Mae said with excitement in her voice. "Hmmm, maybe we do need another boy." Grandma and Daddy listened to the girls talk about their fears and perhaps joy about having another boy in the family. Both Grandma and Daddy knew that this baby was the last. Mama's health was becoming a big risk, having so many children in so few years.

As time for delivery drew near, Granny came to the house to stay with the children while Daddy took Mama to the hospital. Granny wore those blue canvas shoes that she wore for walking. She knew she'd be walking a lot keeping up with the six children. Daddy dressed in his usual jeans and plaid shirt, but this time he was wearing his dress black shoes and carrying a little suitcase with gowns for Mama. A dress and blanket for a baby girl, and if by chance she had a boy, she had a romper outfit. Mama was wearing the biggest dress she had, and even that was too tight. Her feet and ankles

*Marlene Rose*

were swollen so much that you could hardly tell where the bones were. She was very uncomfortable. She was now the biggest she had ever been when she was having all of her babies. The children felt for sure she was having a boy. On her feet she wore bedroom slippers like the ones she wore to the hospital when Anna Grace was sick. The bedroom slippers were the only shoes they had seen her wear lately. Granny looked at her and shook her head. With the little suitcase in one hand, holding on to Mama with the other hand, they went to the car. Still holding on to Mama, Daddy put the suitcase down. He opened the door for Mama to get in to Miss Susie, then carrying the suitcase he opened one of the back doors to put it inside. Next Daddy got in Miss Susie. He started her, and they left for the hospital.

At that moment Anna Grace thought about her Grandpa leaving for the hospital in Mr. Chick's car. She hoped this hospital visit did not end like Grandpa's visit. Then she thought a baby boy wouldn't be so bad after all. Anna Grace and Ellie Mae went to the house, looking over what the new baby would wear. Most of the clothes were for a girl; that's about all they had at the house. None of Billy Bob's clothes would be good enough, because he wore them out at the knees playing cowboys and Indians or sliding down the riverbank while fishing. So maybe Mama didn't know after all if the baby was a girl or boy.

Two days later, she was still in the hospital: no baby yet. Granny looked worried; she never worried about anything, but she was now. Granny was a free spirit. Mama said she would never have wrinkles in her face if worrying caused them.

*Something must be wrong for the delivery to take so long,* the

## Seven, No More

children thought. Ellie Mae with her smart mouth said, "I'll tell you what's wrong. That baby doesn't want to come yet."

Granny asked her, "How do you know so much, young lady? Is it because you have an eighth-grade education? I know that baby will come when the time is right, and I can't write my own name. I didn't go to school, but I understand that babies come when they are ready. Your papa graduated from high school. Maybe you got his brains," Granny replied sarcastically.

Ellie Mae was surprised Granny didn't go to school, because she could do so many things. She could play the harp, banjo, and guitar. *Everyone said she could sing like a mockingbird; perhaps that's where the children got their singing talent,* Ellie Mae thought. With all her talent, Granny could have been famous in one of those bluegrass bands. When she married Papa she was only fifteen years old, and he was twenty-five. Many said he robbed the cradle. He was so taken with her beauty and personality that he wanted her for his wife. Granny had black curly hair, dark eyes, and always a smile on that dark face.

Papa graduated from high school, then moved to her town as the superintendent of the cotton gin. A very powerful job for a man of only twenty-five years, he was single and handsome, with dark straight hair and bright blue eyes. He was on the slight side—about five feet, ten inches in height, and very trim.

All the single girls in town fell for him. Even some of the married ones looked at him two or three times. Papa was a little shy with the ladies, but when he saw Granny all the shyness left. Granny's parents died when she was five years old. Then she went to live with Uncle Jim and his wife. They were tobacco and cotton farmers with little education, but

## Marlene Rose

smart people. Because they never went to school, they didn't think Granny needed to go. They were the kind of people, the children heard Daddy say many times, who would give you the shirt off their backs if you needed it. Little did they know that she would meet this educated man, fall in love, and marry him.

Every time Granny went to the cotton gin with Uncle Jim, the superintendent worked with them. Little did Uncle Jim see what was happening with Granny and Papa. Being the gentleman he was, Papa asked Uncle Jim for permission to marry her. He confessed his love for Granny, and he promised to take care of her.

After listening, Uncle Jim said, "She is only fourteen years old. If you are serious, the two of you can marry when she turns fifteen."

Papa returned to the cotton gin happy and sad—happy that he had permission to marry Granny, sad because they had to wait so long. Daily he counted the months and days off his calendar, looking forward to the next day. Papa saved his money. Before Granny turned fifteen, Papa purchased a big house with columns on the front porch; up over the front porch was a balcony. The house was on thirty acres of land on a rolling hill at the edge of town. Papa filled the house with the finest furniture, rugs, and beautiful linens, and he waited patiently for Granny to turn fifteen. The house had not one, but two toilets. It looked like a picture out of a book.

On Granny's fifteenth birthday, the two of them were married at that house with her Uncle Jim and his wife present. Granny became his wife, his lover, and his lifelong companion, until his death of a heart attack at age fifty-eight.

The lingering Depression robbed him of his home with

## Seven, No More

thirty acres of land. Year after year during the Depression, no money was made on the cotton crops. Therefore the cotton gin had little work. Without work, there was no money, yet the taxes had to be paid. His dearly beloved house and land were sold at public auction, leaving the family to find a place for their fine furnishings and linens. At that time there were three children in the family. Papa wanted them to have a place to call home, so he found a small house for them. All the style of fine living at the house with the fancy parties and dances were behind them. Even their horse and buggy were sold. It was time to walk like a lot of people were doing. It was survival time.

After moving into the house near the cotton gin, he was more content—wanting to be as far away as possible but in the same town as the house and land that were once his home. The memories of selling his house and land in front of the county courthouse at auction stayed with him. Granny said she felt he never got over what he lost. He wanted the very best for his wife (whom he adored) and his children. She was left with the memory of what might have been with her beloved husband. After he died, Granny was faced with taking care of their four children: Daddy, Pete and Sally, and Aunt Bessie. Not having any education, she went to work at the cotton mill as a spinner on the opposite end of town from the mill where Daddy worked. As she needed money, she sold some of her antiques. She said there were still some rich people who were willing to buy what they wanted, and other people who were willing to sell to survive. Some of the rich people got their riches at the expense of others' suffering during the Depression.

Having told the girls about their family, Granny looked at them and said, "Your daddy is just like Papa. He wants the

*Marlene Rose*

best for all of you." About the time Granny finished her story, Daddy drove up in Miss Susie.

Still wondering with excitement, Granny asked, "Son, what is it? Do you have a boy or girl?"

With a smile on his face, a half-smoked cigarette hanging out the corner of his mouth, and with a wrinkled shirt and jeans that looked like he slept in them for days, he replied, "It's a boy! Children, your mama is so happy. She is going to name him Jim, after my Uncle Jim, and we are going to call him Jim Boy."

Granny was so pleased that Mama included her family in his name. Many times Granny did not feel welcome around Mama. Daddy assured her that Mama's mood and attitude had nothing to do with her. It was the middle-child syndrome. Many people can never overcome that borne position in their life, with the feeling of not belonging. Mama worked hard to overcome the middle-child syndrome.

"Son," Granny said, "I am so glad you told me about that syndrome thing. I always felt I couldn't measure up to her."

"I have always enjoyed the children coming to the house to visit, but sometimes she would not let them," Granny told Daddy as the children listened. All of the children loved visiting Granny's house, sitting with her on the front porch overlooking the rock-fenced graveyard where Papa was buried. With Granny playing the banjo and all of them singing, they had lots of fun. Granny had so much talent. *Maybe some of the talent would go to Jim Boy,* they thought. None of the six children could play anything, but they could all sing like Granny.

Mama's delivery of Jim Boy was difficult. She stayed in the hospital five more days; Daddy took the family to see her

## Seven, No More

and Jim Boy. The first thing she said about him was, "I have my preacher man now, and God has answered my prayer."

Ellie Mae spoke up, "Anna Grace and I will train him to be a singing preacher. With all of Granny's musical talents, he will be good. Being he was named for her side of the family, you know she can sing and play anything." Mama just listened.

Billy Bob had to get his two cents in. "I will teach him to be a fisherman just like Daddy did me."

"You can't even catch a turtle coming toward you," said Ellie Mae with contempt in her voice. The two continued badgering each other for a while.

With all the excitement of the new baby, everyone forgot to watch Sara Beth. "Where is she?" Mama started crying. "Somebody has my baby, Sara Beth."

Everyone scrambled from the room looking for her. Unnoticed she slipped out of the room and toddled down the hall to the nurses station, where they found her sitting on the lap of a young handsome doctor, eating, of all things, a lollipop.

As Anna Grace approached him, he said, "I need this one. You already have four other girls. My dear wife wants a little girl so much, this one is perfect—red hair and brown eyes, just like my wife."

"No, no," they all shouted together. "If you want one of us, take the new baby. We are not used to him yet." The doctor just laughed and handed Sara Beth over to Anna Grace. What a relief to find her and get her back.

Within a few days, Mama and the new baby were coming home. Many chores needed to be done to make the house perfect for Mama and baby Jim Boy. Granny was still

*Marlene Rose*

with them; so were Pete and Sally. Everyone with Granny's instructions started cleaning and preparing the house.

With the new baby needing the crib, Sara Beth had to start sleeping somewhere else. "Where do you want to sleep?" Granny asked Sara Beth.

"With my mama," she replied in her little two-year-old voice.

Granny knew Sara Beth needed some special attention since the new baby had come. "We'll see," she replied.

At last Mama and Jim Boy came home from the hospital. Mama was unusually thin and tired after delivering Jim Boy. Mama was thrilled about the new baby boy, but she couldn't take care of him because she was exhausted from childbirth. Granny, Pete, and Sally decided to stay awhile to help Mama with the children. Pete entertained Billy Bob to keep him out of Mama's way. He was so glad she was home that he couldn't stay away from Mama. Sally helped Anna Grace and Ellie Mae with the younger girls. With much concern, Granny watched Mama hold Jim Boy for long periods of time and cry while she rocked him. Then, as if she realized she was holding a new baby in her arms, she looked at him and smiled. Could it be that she was sad that this was her last baby? Sometimes Daddy looked at Jim Boy and just cried. Was there something wrong with this baby boy? Granny assured the children that everything was fine with him. The two of them were sad because there would be no more babies. One of the reasons Mama stayed at the hospital so long and why she was so thin was that she had an operation so she was through with having babies. Early in her pregnancy, the doctor told Daddy, her body was exhausted from childbearing. She didn't need to have another pregnancy. Jim Boy was her last baby!

## Seven, No More

Knowing that Mama wanted Jim Boy for her preacher man, Ellie Mae and Anna Grace were going to train him as a singing preacher. With Granny's talent as a musician, she could teach him to play anything. There was a lot of talent in this family of five girls and now two boys. The love for music could be traced back to Granny. She taught Daddy, and he taught us as toddlers with the one-line songs—"Jesus Loves Me" and "This Little Light of Mine." Much happiness had been brought into the family through music.

Ellie Mae and Anna Grace had become close friends as well as sisters; they always sang together as they completed their chores. Whether it was washing dishes in a blue galvanized dishpan and drying them with hand-knitted towels or cooking, they sang. Anna Grace would set the table and make the ice tea while Ellie Mae made the gravy for the meat. The gravy was made with bacon drippings heated with self-rising flour, stirred until there were no lumps, adding enough water to boil, and then simmering about five minutes. Whatever the two girls did, if it was picking cotton, cleaning the house, or cooking, they sang. At about nine and ten years old, they started singing in public. First they sang at church and camp meetings, and had special invitations to sing. Many times at these special events, a special offering would be taken for them. Ellie Mae sang soprano and Anna Grace sang harmony, mainly because Anna Grace had a stronger voice and added color to Ellie Mae's soprano. After they turned twelve and thirteen years old, they were invited to sing at entertainment functions.

As ninth-graders at high school, they were invited to sing at the senior prom. The performance required evening dresses, which neither of them owned. The family finances were not enough to buy the dresses, so they had to reject the invitation. One of the senior girls was Dr. Jones's daughter. She heard that they couldn't perform because they didn't have evening dresses, so several gowns were offered to them for loan. The night before the performance, Ellie Mae and Anna Grace rolled their hair on strips of rags. Often times, especially on Sundays, they rolled their hair this way to give them that curly, bouncy look. The night of the prom, both girls looked especially beautiful. Anna Grace wore a bright red off-the-shoulder satin gown that made her long curly raven hair and black eyes stand out, while Ellie Mae wore a pale blue strapless gown (she could keep it up) that accentuated her blazing red hair piled up with little curls. Because the gowns were so long, their old high heels didn't show. They sang several songs at the prom that night, but the one song Ellie Mae liked best was "Blue Moon," which was a showstopper. After they finished singing, they received a standing ovation. Upon hearing about that outstanding performance, the director of the high school choir, of which they were members, asked them to sing a duet backed by the sixty voices of the choir on senior night of graduation. The song was the beautiful "Battle Hymn of the Republic." It was exhilarating! The harmony of the two voices just flowed with enthusiasm throughout the auditorium. Afterwards Anna Grace told Ellie Mae that she felt like the windows of heaven opened and all the angels were singing with the choir. With the music and the singing, Anna Grace had trouble keeping her feet still.

Another time that brought excitement to the girls was being invited to sing the opening number at a gospel concert! With great pleasure they accepted, and they sang their hearts out. Looking grown-up in their gray tweed dresses with red knit trim and red leather high heels, the girls took

## Seven, No More

the stage holding handheld mikes for the first time in their lives. They sang like they were pros. The auditorium was filled, as people clapped and tapped their feet to the music. Later Ellie Mae told her sister that she was so scared that she almost started to walk off the stage. Of all the different arenas where they sang, the greatest pleasure was singing in church, whether it was the choir or singing a duet. It was singing praises to God!

# A New Job

With seven children—two boys and five girls—to feed, clothe, and educate, Daddy needed a better-paying job with opportunities. Since Mama had Jim Boy, her health was not as good. Realizing this, Daddy considered whether he should lease the land for the next year. With the land, the family grew their food and planted cotton for the needed extra money. Daddy was so proud that Mama could stay home with the children; all those years working at the mill plus the responsibilities of home had taken a toll on her. He knew the sacrifices the two of them made to make their dream of freedom from debt a reality. Working together, the entire family made this dream come true. Debt-free!

Now it was time for another step to be taken in their life. At the mill Daddy was a good machinist and an excellent welder, but the opportunity for advancement was not there. A man had to be either a member of the mill owner's family or a close friend to advance. Daddy was neither. Deciding it was time for a change, he went to the big city to explore

## Seven, No More

his possibilities. Upon arriving in the city, he started applying at places of employment that interested him. Many times he thought about his family—how his children needed a chance to further their education or better opportunities for employment if higher education was not their choice. Another thing that drew his attention was the schools, colleges, and universities everywhere. Almost anyone could better their education; maybe he could, even though he was thirty-five years old. He could dream!

Being thirty-five years old and experienced in welding and fixing machinery, he didn't have any trouble finding positions available. Many manufacturers were looking for qualified machinists as well as welders, so he applied for both positions at several places. The pay scale and the benefits were better than the mill. Would it be economical for them to live there? After applying for the job positions, Daddy went home excited and encouraged about the future. Both Mama and Daddy decided to lease the land for one more year. If Daddy got a job, he would commute. Because the cotton money was helping them to stay debt-free, they could sacrifice a little while longer.

Within five days after he applied, he received a letter from a foundry company that wanted to interview him. Daddy was so excited that he had trouble speaking. Finally after reading the letter again, he called for an appointment, which was scheduled for the next week.

To the foundry Daddy went for his interview. Daddy's appearance was very businesslike, dressed in a navy blue sports coat with khaki pants, and coordinated with a red, navy, and camel–colored tie and brown lace-up dress shoes. His natural curly black hair was neatly trimmed and brushed into place, and he had a smile on his face showing his bright,

*Marlene Rose*

white, even teeth. Mama made sure he looked appropriate. As he entered the room, the interviewer extended his hand, smiled, and offered Daddy a chair across the table from him.

Introducing himself as the interviewer, Tom Waters was a tall, thin man in his early forties with full salt-and-pepper hair, dressed in a dark gray suit with a coordinating red and blue tie with scattered gray dots. He was immaculate in appearance, and his pleasant personality showed with his smile, making Daddy feel at ease.

Mr. Waters started with his questions: "Why are you interested in leaving your old job of thirteen years?" "During the war you worked at the shipyard as a welder for four years. Is that right?" he asked.

Daddy explained he had seven children. He wanted more opportunities for them than he could provide for them while working at the mill.

Mr. Waters looked puzzled. Looking at the application again, then looking at Daddy, he said, "Your application lists six children. Have you added another child since then?"

"No," Daddy replied. "Will you read off the names so I can correct my application?"

Mr. Waters started reading the names, "Anna Grace, Lilly Lee, Ellie Mae, Billy Bob, Sara Beth, and Jim Boy."

"Oh my," Daddy said. "How could I leave out Holly Rose? She is the sweetest little girl with blond curly hair always knotted and big brown eyes. She looks like my sister Barb. Both of them just love animals, especially cats. Sometimes she visits our neighbor, Mr. Weathers, to play with his cat, Lucy. Mr. Weathers is concerned that Holly Rose will hurt Lucy, and if he sees her coming, he puts Lucy in the house, telling Holly Rose she is taking a nap. Enough said."

## Seven, No More

Mr. Waters looked at him and asked, "Are there any more little ones on the way?"

Daddy replied, "That Jim Boy would be the last. Mama is not healthy enough to have any more children." With that question answered, he shook Daddy's hand, thanked him for the interview, and told him he would hear something soon. Daddy wondered, *When is soon?*

As Daddy started to leave the office, a bald-headed, well-dressed gentleman in a navy suit in the reception room stopped him, saying, "With all those children, I know what you have been doing in your spare time."

Angrily, Daddy returned a stare. Then, as if something came over him, he smiled and said, "You're right, and God has blessed me!"

That night after supper, Daddy told Mama about the interview. Both of them laughed about forgetting his children's name. "You probably got their ages wrong too," Mama said, laughing uncontrollably. Afterwards, he told her about the man in the front office.

"I'm so glad you didn't lose your temper. You could have destroyed your chance of getting that job. Many times I've seen you lose your temper when people start asking you about the number of children you have. You get real offensive. You shouldn't, because it is an absolute blessing to have these children." Daddy agreed!

In about two weeks, Daddy got a letter from the foundry telling him the job was his. If he accepted, a pay scale and benefit package would follow. With his experience, he could start midway up the pay scale. Thrilled at the news, he could hardly wait to accept the job. The pay was more than his job at the mill after thirteen years of employment. At the end of the letter was, "P.S. I am sorry I embarrassed you as you were leaving the office. You are a man of impeccable character. Please forgive me." Daddy didn't know who this person was, but he must have been important.

Within the next week, he accepted the job, turned into his supervisor his notice of leaving, and started getting Miss Susie ready to travel. Miss Susie would be getting a new parking space and probably enjoy spending time with Daddy on the road. Lilly Lee would miss polishing Miss Susie's headlights every other day. She was very worried about Miss Susie being able to see in the dark, because Lilly Lee knew that Daddy would be driving in the dark sometimes.

On October 1, Daddy started his new job at the foundry. Early every morning, he'd put on his clean jeans, plaid shirt, and combat boots, and head to work. Two other things he would not forget were his Bible and his cigarettes. He was a cigarette-smoking, Bible-reading man. At lunchtime while eating, he read his Bible. Several of the men wanted him to read aloud. At first Daddy hesitated, thinking they were making fun of him. Then he realized that maybe they were like Granny, and they couldn't read. So after he ate, Daddy read to them.

On Saturday everyone in the family had a chore to do in the field. They all gathered their golden pumpkins for selling. Because they lived on a main highway, cars would stop and inquire about the beautiful golden-orange pumpkins in the front yard.

Halloween was drawing near, and most families wanted a pumpkin to carve. They had all sizes: little, medium, big, and extra-big pumpkins. The crop was bountiful that year. About a week before Halloween on Saturday, plus every evening after school, they sold pumpkins. No selling on Sunday, though: Mama told them to come back another day. "That's

## Seven, No More

the Lord's day," she would say. Anna Grace thought to herself: *Every day is the Lord's day, isn't it?*

After Halloween, they continued to sell pumpkins until Thanksgiving. By that time the harvest was getting low. The family worked hard during the pumpkin season and made lots of money for Christmas.

That Thanksgiving was wonderful. Grandma and Mr. Farris came, bringing a big ham already cooked and some pumpkin pies (the pumpkins came from the family). Granny came, with Pete and Sally bringing her specialty: pecan pies and blueberry shortcake. Mama cooked a turkey and a meatloaf from ground beef and sausage, and they had all kinds of vegetables from the garden. Anna Grace had learned to make biscuits as well as her famous sweet ice tea. Ellie Mae made some of her good gravy. What a feast!

Mama invited Mr. Weathers for Thanksgiving dinner. As usual, he ate without talking. The children stared at him, and he stared back. Occasionally someone would ask him a direct question; he'd answer one word, then back to eating. *It must be hard living alone with just your cat and dog,* the children thought. After Mr. Weathers finished eating, he sat there while everyone else ate, and once in a while he would belch. He said nothing.

After dinner Mr. Weathers went home without saying thank-you, but that didn't bother Mama. She was used to him being rude, but she still sent food for his big black dog.

Grandma said, "I have never seen anyone like him."

Granny replied, "He doesn't know any better since he has lived alone so long."

"Maybe," said Mr. Farris, "but he gives me the creeps."

The weather cooperated, cool but sunny. The children played outside after dinner. The big ones played horseshoes with Daddy and Mr. Farris, while the little ones played ring around the roses before playing in the dirt.

Everyone was having fun, even the women working in the kitchen—talking, cleaning, and washing dishes.

Anna Grace didn't remember another time that Daddy was able to spend Thanksgiving without going to the mill.

The family enjoyed a very happy Thanksgiving!

# Mama Goes to the Dentist

After the birth of Jim Boy and her operation, Mama went through menopause, causing the family a lot of pain and suffering, Mama also started having toothaches. Without having much money, she neglected her dental check-ups with Dr. Chew, although Daddy and the children continued their visits every two years with the good Dr. Chew.

Mama talked to Grandma about the problems with her teeth. Immediately Grandma said, "Daughter, have you not heard that every baby takes a tooth? That statement is partly true because each pregnancy pulls calcium from the mother for the baby, and we need calcium for our teeth. In my early days, we didn't have that fancy toothpaste. We used salt and baking soda to brush our teeth. Not very good-tasting toothpaste, but the best cleaner. Choosing not to use the salt and soda mixture, I chose not to care for my teeth. As a result of that choice, I lost a lot of my own teeth. I have teeth, but they are false. Perhaps that's why so many women have false

*Marlene Rose*

teeth. The more children they have, the fewer teeth they have left, especially if they have not used good dental care."

Mama stared at Grandma in disbelief, and then she asked, "Is that why you have false teeth? You only had four children, and you lost your teeth?"

Grandma answered, "I didn't take care of my teeth. Please be aware it can happen to you too."

Mama began to worry about the number of teeth she might lose. At the young age of thirty-five, she wondered if false teeth were ahead for her. Losing seven teeth could prove a hardship in biting or eating her food. What if she lost those seven teeth up front? Mama might look like the Halloween jack-o-lanterns she warned the children about if they continued eating candy.

Aunt Grace had false teeth, but she was at least ninety years old. Looking at Anna Grace and the other children as they slept, she thought out loud, "How will these children feel about their mama wearing false teeth after all the complaining about them eating candy?"

She and Daddy made sure their children continued with good dental care. They brushed their teeth every morning and night, and they visited Dr. Chew once every two years. That was the best they could do with all those children. Mama insisted they eat fruits and vegetables with very little candy. So cavities were kept to a minimum, with Daddy and Billy Bob never having a cavity. Could it be that only boys had cavity-free teeth?

With Mama having a toothache and needing to see Dr. Chew, Daddy encouraged her to come with him and the children for their regular visit. After deciding the dental visit was a good idea, they piled in Miss Susie for a trip to Dr. Chew's office. In the front seat with Mama was Jim Boy, with

## Seven, No More

Daddy driving Miss Susie. Located in the back seat was Ellie Mae holding Sara Beth; Billy Bob next to Ellie Mae, punching her as he sat down; then Lilly Lee and Anna Grace with Holly Rose holding down the hump. As these children grew bigger, Daddy would seem to need to buy a bus. Anna Grace thought that Miss Susie would be sad when that happens.

With Billy Bob punching Ellie Mae every time she glanced away, finally Ellie Mae, holding her fist in his face, asked him, "Do you want some false teeth like Grandma?"

Billy Bob hollered for Mama to make Ellie Mae stop bad-mouthing him.

Instead Mama said, "Anna Grace, change places with him." That put him beside Lilly Lee, sitting next to the door. If Lilly Lee punched him, out the door he'd go. He decided to be good until the trip home. He wasn't ready for false teeth.

The town had one dentist, Dr. Chew, who was the daddy of their friends Kate and Jane when they lived in town. Dr. Chew was a tall, thin man with some balding around his forehead. Anna Grace thought the balding might be the result of that headgear thing he wore when he looked in your mouth. Daddy said those were dental glasses: he could see like a magnifying glass. As he pulled the glasses from his head, they probably shaved some of that hair off. Dr. Chew always wore a white doctor jacket over his regular clothes. He looked like a real doctor, like the ones they saw in hospitals.

As they went in Dr. Chew's office, Anna Grace asked Mama, "Do you want to be first or last?"

Mama replied in a tone of anguish, "I don't know, maybe somewhere in between. Are you going first, Anna Grace?"

Looking at Mama, Anna Grace could see she was afraid,

so she answered, "Yes, I will be first, since I am the oldest and I need to set a good example."

Into Dr. Chew's office Anna Grace went. He examined her teeth, saying no cavities.

Next Billy Bob wanted to see Dr. Chew. He was still worried about Ellie Mae knocking out his teeth. Dr. Chew said he had a good check-up: excited, he went back into the waiting room, showing his new toothbrush and saying to Mama, "Why don't you go next? He is giving out good reports."

Mama looked at him and just smiled, saying, "I knew you would get a good report, but I won't. I have decided to be last."

One by one, each child had the check-up. Everyone had a good report, including Daddy. Now it was Mama's turn. Looking scared, she went in Dr. Chew's office. While all the children were peeping around the corner into his office, he took that little eyeglass off his head, looking at Mama's teeth. He shook his head. "You need to take better care of your teeth. You have done a good job with those children. If you don't start now, in ten years or less, you'll be wearing false teeth," said Dr. Chew.

All that information went straight to Mama's heart. She would do better by her teeth.

After the examination, everybody got in Miss Susie to go home. The riding arrangement was the same, except Billy Bob was riding on the hump. With all the girls around him, he didn't have a chance to be anything but good.

# Planning for Christmas
## (Buying Presents)

Soon after Thanksgiving, they started planning for Christmas: buying presents, cutting the tree, decorating the tree and the house, and making the cookies. Daddy was taking the children shopping the first Saturday in December. They were so excited, and so was Daddy. Each of them had ten dollars to spend on presents for family and friends—money they made selling pumpkins. All week long they were planning what they would buy and who they would buy for. Ten dollars was a lot of money. They knew they could buy a lot with that much money. Selling all those pumpkins made them happy—giving them Christmas money and making those people happy who bought them for Halloween.

Anna Grace made list upon list, which she changed daily, while Ellie Mae kept asking everyone, "What do you want for Christmas?" hoping someone would ask her, but no one did.

Ellie Mae could never make up her mind about anything, let alone how to spend her ten dollars.

## Marlene Rose

Billy Bob, as Grandma often said, was a case in action. There was no one in the world like him; the first person he would always think about was Billy Bob. Once while shopping with Mama at the five-and-dime store, he saw a gun and holster he wanted real bad. "Maybe I'll buy that first," he said.

So excited was Lilly Lee that she could hardly contain herself, knowing what she was going to buy: Mama and Daddy—a gift together; Grandma and Mr. Farris—a gift together; Pete, Sally, and Granny—a gift together; and then wondering if she could do the same for Anna Grace and Ellie Mae, but she decided against that.

Poor Holly Rose didn't want to spend her ten dollars on anyone except Sara Beth. She knew Sara Beth would let her play with anything she had. She knew they could use some new toys, but she decided to buy a present for everyone. That was the fair thing to do, because everyone was buying her a present. Maybe someone would buy her that doll she wanted so much, but did they know which doll?

Daddy was helping Sara Beth choose her presents. She was too young to understand that her ten dollars was for spending. Poor, poor Jim Boy: he was much too young to give ten dollars. Maybe Santa would bring him something that cost ten dollars.

Every night Daddy watched with amazement as the children planned their Christmas shopping trip. Excitement filled the family from the biggest to the littlest.

Saturday came, and off they went to town in Miss Susie. Daddy and Billy Bob were in the front; holding down the back seat were the five girls, with Sara Beth sitting on the middle hump this time. Finally Anna Grace had someone else sitting on the hump.

Arriving in town, they headed to the five-and-dime store,

## Seven, No More

each going in different directions. Ellie Mae headed off to the china area: no luck there, everything cost too much for her. She wandered over to the candy counter, deciding candy would rot the teeth. "So what in the world can I buy for my family?" she said out loud.

The salesperson heard and said, "How much money do you have?"

Ellie Mae replied with enthusiasm, "Why, I have ten dollars, so I can buy a lot of presents."

Anna Grace overheard Ellie Mae and the salesperson. She thought that Ellie Mae can't decide anything. Anna Grace had her list of everything to buy with its cost, while Ellie Mae wanted to look around to see what was available.

Excited, Billy Bob said he would buy everyone a present after he bought his own.

Lilly Lee was busy counting her money after she bought her presents. She had money left! Holly Rose was admiring this pretty little doll dressed in pink for Sara Beth; she knew she could play with it. Looking around, Anna Grace saw Daddy helping Sara Beth choose her presents.

Sara Beth kept saying, "I want this for Mama."

Lilly Lee turned, saying to the others, "She's a real mama's girl."

Holly Rose, wanting to know, asked, "What's wrong with that?"

Looking at his watch, Daddy saw that the store would be closing soon. Even though there were six people spending ten dollars each, the store would be closing in ten minutes.

Daddy called to the children, "Meet me at the front door in five minutes. You have just enough time to pay for your purchases." Immediately Lilly Lee, Anna Grace, and Holly Rose met Daddy at the front door. He was standing, holding

*Marlene Rose*

Sara Beth with her bag of presents. Ellie Mae was still looking around, but where was Billy Bob? All of a sudden, he appeared with a sack full of presents for everyone, including Mr. Weathers.

"What did you buy yourself?" Ellie Mae busted out. "I know you bought for yourself first."

"I didn't have enough money left for me. I had to buy my friend Big Black Dog something."

"Some friend you are," said Ellie Mae in her bossy voice. "You are always chasing that dog with a stick. Mr. Weathers gets so angry with you chasing his dog."

"Oh, I bought Mr. Weathers something too," Billy Bob replied. "He's a real nice man."

Lilly Lee spoke up, "Don't worry about not getting a present. I bought you something."

As they started home, excited and fatigued, Billy Bob, sitting in the front seat with Daddy, said, "That was a good shopping trip."

All the girls in the back agreed, except Sara Beth. She was laying in Anna Grace's arms fast asleep, not on the hump in the middle. Daddy told them, "The secret of Christmas is surprise! So don't tell anyone anything." Everyone knew Ellie Mae would tell everyone what she bought. She couldn't keep a secret!

Arriving at home, all the children ran to show Mama their bags of presents, but she could not look inside. Everyone had fun shopping with their ten dollars.

"It's a surprise," they all shouted together!

# "One Tree"

"Next Saturday is tree-cutting time," said Daddy. "Everyone needs to get their chores done early. That includes you, Billy Bob."

All week long, every afternoon, Billy Bob spent time making a sled to pull the Christmas tree home, using Daddy's hammer, nails, saw, and leftover scrap wood. Bringing a rope from his house, Mr. Weathers fastened the rope on the sled, allowing them to pull it.

"Brilliant, Billy Bob," said Daddy.

Saturday finally came; six of the seven children dressed warmly as they went Christmas tree–looking in the woods. Anna Grace and Ellie Mae helped Holly Rose and Sara Beth find warm coats, pants, scarves, and gloves from the hand-me-down closet. Looking inside herself, Lilly Lee found a warm coat, hat, and gloves that once belonged to Anna Grace, so they were in excellent condition. Anna Grace was particular about her clothes. After she outgrew them, they still looked brand-new, but not Ellie Mae's clothes. Mama said, "She is hard on her clothes. About the only thing that they are good for is scrubbing the floors."

Being the only boy for a long time, Billy Bob's outgrown clothes were in the closet for Jim Boy. All of them looked alike, just different colors and sizes, just like Daddy and Billy Bob. Billy Bob and Daddy made sure they wore gloves. Those Christmas trees had thorns sometimes, especially if you cut a holly tree.

Heading to the woods with Sara Beth riding on the sled, everyone went. Looking around at all the trees, each of the children wanted to cut a different tree, but Daddy said, "One tree."

Finally they came to a thicket in the woods with all kinds of trees: big ones, little ones, thick ones, skinny ones, thorny ones, and most of all, beautiful ones. While Daddy was watching all the children, they were running wild, with even little Sara Beth following behind, screaming, "I want that one."

Anna Grace was busy looking for the tree. She came upon a beautiful green pine with long pine needles and pinecones. With colored lights, garlands, and ribbons, she thought they could have the most beautiful Christmas tree in the world. As Billy Bob and Ellie Mae were walking together, they spotted some different-looking trees. Billy Bob thought the holly tree with red berries and shiny glossy leaves looked like a Christmas tree. Never mind that the leaves were thorny. It would be hard to string lights and hang garland on a tree like that, so he passed over the tree.

In the meantime, behind him, Ellie Mae was shouting, "I've found the perfect tree."

It had sharply loaded leaves with prickly clusters standing about six feet tall. It was called a sweet-gum tree. Billy

# Seven, No More

Bob mentioned to her that you would not need many decorations; maybe some colored lights with those little balls already on the tree. Sara Beth wanted a big hog apple tree (hawthorn), so they could hang lots of gumdrops on it like the one she saw at Mr. Farris's store.

Ellie Mae told her, "Those gumdrops were not real. Besides, we can't hang lighted decorations on the tree."

Small as she was, Sara Beth didn't understand; she started to cry. Lilly Lee spoke up and said, "I bet Daddy will let you have a small hog apple tree filled with gumdrops for the kitchen table. Let's ask him."

Before they could ask, Holly Rose hollered at the top of her voice, "I've found it. I've found the perfect tree."

Daddy and the rest of them went running to see the perfect tree. The tree was an evergreen with short green thistle scratchy needles in clusters forming a leaflike appearance. It stood between six and seven feet tall. Simply put—just beautiful—a cedar tree! All the girls were jumping with joy, while Daddy and Billy Bob started cutting down the tree. All the while Anna Grace and Ellie Mae were talking how beautiful it would be decorated for Christmas and watching the smaller children at the same time. Daddy and Billy Bob continued cutting the tree.

The tree fell. Wearing gloves to protect their hands, Daddy and Billy Bob lifted the tree onto the sled. Grabbing the rope that Mr. Weathers and Billy Bob attached to the sled, Daddy started pulling.

Just before they got home, Anna Grace said, "We need a wreath for the front door."

Daddy said, "We will cut down that small holly tree yonder. You, Mama, and the girls can make a wreath. With the red berries on the holly and a red bow, it will be outstanding!"

While they were gathering the small holly tree, Ellie Mae found some mistletoe, but they didn't need it since none of them had sweethearts. No kissing at this house unless it was Mama and Daddy.

Lilly Lee told Daddy about Sara Beth wanting a gumdrop tree. He found a small hawthorn tree just big enough for the table. Adding the little tree and trimmings to the sled, Billy Bob continued pulling the full sled home, while Sara Beth rode on Daddy's shoulders.

Mama was thrilled with their finds!

# Decorating the Tree

After church the next day, the family hurried home to decorate the Christmas tree. Daddy put the cedar tree in a bucket with dirt and water. Daddy packed the dirt around the tree so it would not turn over with Jim Boy and Sara Beth playing around it. While Mama was stringing the color lights from the year before, Anna Grace and Ellie Mae were helping Sara Beth and Holly Rose make paper garlands out of red and white construction paper. They showed them how to cut one-inch strips and circle them with paste, one after another, until they made a long string to go around the tree from top to bottom. Daddy observed Sara Beth had more paste on her than the garland she was making.

Always a helper, Holly Rose told Sara Beth, "Let me show you how to string them."

That didn't go over well because the paste had not dried. The garland fell apart. So they assigned Lilly Lee to help. She was good at using paste and cutting one-inch strips out of colored paper. She was also good at stopping little girls from

*Marlene Rose*

cutting each others' hair. Bored, Ellie Mae moved on to stringing the popcorn that Mama popped while they were getting the tree. Fumbling with a needle and thread, she tried to string the popcorn. After stringing one bowl of popcorn, she quit. She was ready for something else.

"Where's Billy Bob?" she asked Daddy.

"He's outside picking up pine cones to hang on the tree. I'm going to string them for him," Daddy replied.

After Billy Bob brought the pine cones into the house, Daddy started stringing, using a needle and red thread while Billy Bob went visiting.

Jim Boy was too small to do anything. He just toddled around the tree and smiled. This was going to be his second Christmas.

After a long time, Daddy started missing his fishing partner. Billy Bob had gone to Mr. Weathers's house, maybe to play with Big Black Dog or just to visit. Billy Bob told him about their Christmas tree and how much fun they had picking it out.

Suddenly Billy Bob said, "Mr. Weathers, do you have your Christmas tree?"

Mr. Weathers replied, "I don't celebrate Christmas anymore since Mama died. She has been dead twenty years. All the decorations are in the box just like she put them," Mr. Weathers said.

Billy Bob explained later to the family, "His mama loved Christmas and the family gatherings. He misses all of that. Maybe it's time for him to break out of his shell after twenty years. We will have a barbecue soon."

Billy Bob looked at Mr. Weathers and said, "Do you think she had an angel we might borrow?"

Mr. Weathers looked in that funny way with his blue eyes

## Seven, No More

glaring and said, "I don't know, but we will find out." While Mr. Weathers pulled the box from under the bed, looking through everything, they found an angel. Mr. Weathers handed the angel to him and said, "Take it, and put it on your tree." Looking sad at the things in the box, he put the top on and closed it tight.

Leaving with the angel clutched tight in his hands, Billy Bob went home. With Daddy's help, he put the angel on top of the tree: a wonderful place for an angel that had been in a box for twenty years. She had center stage now! What a great man Mr. Weathers was!

# Christmas Eve and Christmas Day

All the children gathered around Daddy every night to look at the Sears-Roebuck catalog. From the smallest girl Sara Beth to the oldest Anna Grace, they picked out what they wanted Santa to bring. Mama said, "You need to choose one special item."

Granny was there one night for dinner; she heard the excitement of the children and wondered how she could help with Christmas.

Being four years old, Sara Beth was so excited, she wanted everything. She and Holly Rose tore a page from the book, carrying the page everywhere they went. The two of them were so excited that they could hardly wait for Christmas.

One morning Sara Beth asked Mama, "Could we burn the Christmas tree lights all the time, just in case Santa wants to come early?" Taking up the conversation, Daddy said, "Santa will come on Christmas Eve, no matter how many lights we burn." He was explaining to her without telling her

## Seven, No More

the lights were too expensive to burn all the time. Christmas Eve was ten days away. The excitement was really growing. Every day Sara Beth wanted to know if this was the day. Finally Daddy got a calendar, marking off every day for Sara Beth and Holly Rose.

On the morning of Christmas Eve, with Mama cooking Christmas dinner, Anna Grace, Ellie Mae, and Lilly Lee were helping Holly Rose and Sara Beth wrap their presents, trying to be careful so no one knew what they were going to get. Daddy had said that the secret of Christmas is the surprise. Billy Bob was wrapping his presents. He had them laying out for everyone to see: Big Black Dog—a red dog collar; Mr. Weathers—gloves, because he had terrible-looking hands; Holly Rose and Lilly Lee—hair bows to keep the hair out of their eyes; Sara Beth—some lollipops; Ellie Mae—a wash cloth, to wash out her foul mouth; Anna Grace—colored paper: for Mama and Daddy—a beautiful Christmas card.

After supper, Christmas Eve, everyone gathered around Daddy while he read the Christmas story from the Bible about the birth of Jesus, being born in a manger.

Next Anna Grace read *The Night Before Christmas,* looking at the excited faces glowing from the Christmas tree. Then the family sang "Silent Night" and "Jingle Bells" in perfect harmony.

For Santa, they put homemade cookies and milk by the Christmas tree on a little lighted lamp table. With all of the excitement in the air, Holly Rose and Sara Beth were shouting "Merry Christmas" and "Goodnight" as they ran to bed! After the two little girls left the room for bed, one by one the older children exited the room. Billy Bob was so excited he could hardly say goodnight while Lilly Lee went running

*Marlene Rose*

up to Daddy, thanking him for taking them to buy the presents for Christmas and for the beautiful Christmas tree.

Ellie Mae just looked at Daddy and said, "Is there really a Santa, or are you fooling us?"

Ellie Mae was always unsure about herself and everything. She never even understood why people were good to each other. Without further conversation, Anna Grace grabbed Ellie Mae by the arm, saying to her, "It's time for bed."

Ellie Mae hesitated but decided to go to bed after waiting for Daddy to give her an answer.

Daddy reminded her that "the secret of Christmas is surprise."

Leaving the Christmas lights burning brightly, Mama and Daddy waited for Santa to bring surprises for each child. As each child fell asleep, Santa stopped by, leaving presents wrapped for everyone. There were two big presents: one for Holly Rose and one for Sara Beth, wrapped in Santa paper tied with red ribbon. On the floor under the tree was a long box with Lilly Lee's name. Standing near the back of the lighted tree were two boxes tied together: a long box and a square box with Billy Bob's name written across them. Beside Billy Bob's present was a red radio flyer wagon with a tag saying "Jim Boy."

Under the tree were two small boxes: one for Ellie Mae and one for Anna Grace. Good things come in small packages, so they say.

The lights on the Christmas tree went out. Christmas morning would soon be upon them.

As the clock struck 6:00 A.M., noises came from all over the house.

Throughout the house there were screams and shouts of

## Seven, No More

joy. "Whoopee!" "Look what Santa brought me!" "Oh, I can't believe it." "Hey, look at this." Everywhere throughout the house there was excitement. There were shouts of joy from the littlest to the biggest.

Ellie Mae was looking under the tree for her name. "What's this?" she said. "A gold bracelet just like Granny's bracelet."

Anna Grace was looking, thinking how could they afford such an expensive piece of jewelry? A sterling silver bracelet, maybe but not gold, but Granny was generous. Continuing to look around, Anna Grace looked at Sara Beth. She was holding tight her little doll wrapped in a pink blanket. She was talking to her doll. Sitting beside Sara Beth was Holly Rose, changing her doll's clothes. She would put new clothes on and put the old clothes in a little suitcase. Both girls were having the time of their life.

Reminiscing, Anna Grace remembered her first doll, when she was about Sara Beth's age. Grandpa got the doll out of the trash just for her, and Mama made doll clothes for her out of scraps from Anna Grace's dresses. Grandpa used to say, "Anna Grace, I would buy you the world if I just had the money." Remembering this, Anna Grace started unwrapping her present, thinking how much she enjoyed the doll Grandpa found for her. He promised that one day she would be big enough to have a watch like Grandma. She admired that watch, and Grandma was never late. "Oh, it's a watch. My very own watch." Anna Grace screamed with excitement.

"No excuse now for being late," said Ellie Mae. Still excited and thrilled about the watch, Anna Grace looked to see what Lilly Lee had opened.

Lilly Lee was seven years old now, and music was her

love. Santa brought her a guitar because Granny was teaching her to play. Who knows—before long Lilly Lee might be playing in one of those bluegrass bands? While Lilly Lee was strumming away, Anna Grace heard Billy Bob screaming at the top of his voice.

"I got it, I got it," he shouted.

"What did you get?" asked Ellie Mae.

"Santa brought me a new rod and reel with a real tackle box: it has everything except maybe the worms," Billy Bob replied.

"With all of that fine gear, maybe now you can catch that turtle," Ellie Mae said with her head turned sideways, glancing back at Billy Bob.

Little Jim Boy was not two years old yet, but Santa didn't forget him. He was playing around on the floor with blocks and balls, putting them in his new red wagon. With all the excitement of everyone opening gifts, Mama and Daddy smiled with joy because each child was so happy.

Daddy thought of Mr. Weathers being alone at Christmas. He turned to Mama, asking, "Do we have enough to share?"

Mama knew he meant food, presents, and love. She said, "Yes."

Along with Billy Bob, with his presents for Big Black Dog and Mr. Weathers, Daddy went to invite him for Christmas dinner.

All the kids thought, *Christmas was great at our house!*

# After Christmas

After the Christmas holiday, everyone was settling in their own routine. Leaving very early every morning with Miss Susie, Daddy would wear a short man-made fur-lined jacket and cap, with a cigarette hanging out the side of his mouth half-smoked, with his Bible and lunch on the front seat, always wearing those heavy combat boots with the steel toes. He traveled thirty miles to work at his new job. He enjoyed his new job and he made new friends, among them a young black man named Dwight. Daddy read from the Bible out loud to Dwight every day at lunch. Dwight, who could not read, was thrilled someone would read to him, especially the Bible.

Every morning while waiting for the yellow school bus with noses turning red, and feet and hands tingling from the cold, the children talked about snow. The temperature was very cold. If it snowed, it would stay for a while, which was fine with them. Sara Beth cried every morning to go to school; she wanted to ride that yellow school bus with Holly

## Marlene Rose

Rose. She missed playing with her so much. She didn't want to play with Jim Boy, because he was only a baby.

Sometime in the middle of January on a Saturday night, the children got their wish. It snowed . . . all night Saturday, all Sunday, and into the night. Twelve inches on the ground, and everything was closing. School and Daddy's work closed too. The roads were heavy with snow, and no one was traveling them. It was almost like having another Christmas holiday but without the presents.

The next morning the kids woke up early to play in the snow. Billy Bob and Daddy went to check on Mr. Weathers. Upon reaching Mr. Weathers's house, Daddy saw some old inner tubes laying in the yard half covered with snow. *Those inner tubes would make good sleds,* Daddy thought to himself. Mr. Weathers had more junk in his yard, commodes from neighbors and friends—just about anything you could imagine that needed to be discarded. Give it to Mr. Weathers!

Billy Bob saw a big black pot sitting on bricks outside filled with melting snow. He thought that was Big Black Dog's water bowl, but Daddy informed him the bowl was for boiling water. Some people who work outside have very dirty clothes. Since all the water that comes from the well is cold, the water has to be boiled to clean the clothes. With hot water and lye soap, anything will get clean.

"Usually," he said, being very patient with Billy Bob, "the man of the house builds a fire under the black pot to heat the water. The pot is called a wash pot for who knows why? It is mainly to heat water.

"During the Great Depression and for a while afterwards, Grandma use to make lye soap in them," Daddy said.

Billy Bob said, still wondering, "Still looks like Big Black Dog's water bowl to me."

## Seven, No More

Interesting enough, but that's not why they came. They wanted to make sure Mr. Weathers was all right, and to borrow an inner tube after they saw he had one.

Answering the door, Mr. Weathers was wearing a heavy army-green overcoat with a fur-lined cap. Billy Bob looked at Mr. Weathers's untied heavy combat boots, hoping the strings didn't trip him. Billy Bob thought he looked like he had been to war in the cold country. Daddy asked, "Are you all right, Mr. Weathers?"

"No, I am about to freeze to death with all this snow. I have a red hot fire going in my potbelly stove, but this house is still cold and I am cold too," Mr. Weathers said, snarling with his blue eyes turning green. "Don't know why we have snow this time of the year. It should come at Christmastime, while everyone is at home."

Daddy invited him over to the house, but Mr. Weathers declined, explaining that he might fall and break something. Billy Bob looked at Mr. Weathers, wondering what he could break wearing all those clothes, especially the untied boots.

As they were leaving, Billy Bob asked Mr. Weathers if he could have one of his inner tubes. Mr. Weathers told him to take as many as he wanted. Only Billy Bob could do that. Mr. Weathers did like that Billy Bob, they were buddies. He liked Daddy too.

Carrying the tubes home, both of them were excited because they were going sledding with the inner tubes.

Billy Bob said, "Mr. Weathers has too much junk around and in his house. Why doesn't he clean up the junk, Mama?"

Before Mama could answer, Daddy replied, "If I had a little more time I would help him clean up that junk."

Then Mama replied in her matter-of-fact voice, "He wouldn't let you move a thing. He has too many memories

*Marlene Rose*

tied to them. That may be all he has without any family. Memories!"

Finally with begging from the family, Mama said she would go sledding with them. Some snow and ice melted the day before, and then during the night it froze again. As Mama started outside, she slid across the ice all the way to the clothesline, breaking her slide as she grabbed the clothesline post. It was too late then. She fell and broke her right arm. Right behind her Daddy and the children slid, but none of them fell. With Daddy helping, she was trying to get up without falling again. She pulled him on the ground in the snow. The two of them started laughing, and the children joined in.

All of them decided to be careful after Mama's fall, but they still went sledding with the tubes. Anna Grace and Sara Beth, Ellie Mae with Holly Rose, while Billy Bob and Lilly Lee each had their own tube, screaming as they rolled down the embankments near the highway. Holding Jim Boy, Daddy watched as they had fun in the snow. Mama complained about pain but wouldn't get out in the snow for fear she would break her other arm. In a couple of days with the snow melting on the roads, Daddy took Mama to see Dr. Jones. One look at her arm, he knew she needed a cast for her broken arm. Dr. Jones could do anything—even cast a broken arm!

After the snow melted some more, Daddy went back to work, driving Miss Susie. Daddy was real careful with Miss Susie; he didn't want her injured. They had enough injures at home with Mama!

# Mama's Sickness

Spring came early that year. Everything was budding and flowering in the yard. Birds were singing and building nests for their little ones. Yellow daffodils and purple tulips lined the path to the front door, with white dogwoods and red cherry trees scattered about in the yard. It was a beautiful sight to behold.

Daddy started breaking the land before the vegetables and cotton were to be planted. It was the same cycle year after year. Breaking land, planting, weeding, and harvesting, but this year was different. With Daddy's new job and the money saved from the past year plus this year's savings, they looked to a free and better life. Daddy was looking forward to finding that for his family.

Toward the end of summer, Mama was getting short tempered and agitated a lot. On Saturdays as Daddy and the children were working in the field—harvesting the vegetables and weeding the cotton—Mama would become agitated with them. Many times she refused to help them; she

*Marlene Rose*

would say she was treated like a slave. None of them could do anything to please her except Sara Beth and Jim Boy. Sara Beth was her baby girl and Jim Boy was her baby boy. She was continually showing motherly love for the two little ones. She seemed to want them to stay small. Oftentimes she would sit in the swing between Sara Beth and Jim Boy, feverishly swinging them and singing for hours. At other times she'd hold Jim Boy, rocking him and crying as if someone was taking him from her. Daddy seemed worried about her, so one Saturday he talked to Dr. Jones. He told Daddy that depression and anxiety comes many times after women finish childbearing naturally. Dr. Jones called this menopause. Since Mama had surgery to stop the childbearing, the depression and anxiety could be more dramatic and fearful—because surgery causes a sudden stop rather than the natural progression. Perhaps she needed some hormone therapy. Most of the time, the problem with depression, anxiety, and fear would ease with hormone pills. He suggested Mama come for blood work soon.

Grandma was worried because she thought Mama might be having a nervous breakdown. Some aunt of hers had a breakdown after menopause. It might be hereditary.

Granny thought it might be the middle child syndrome that Daddy had talked to her about, but Daddy thought she was better with that.

All the children just wanted her to get some doctoring. Dr. Jones could fix anything!

"Nothing is wrong with me except fatigue. You try cooking, cleaning, washing, ironing and caring for these children; you may be depressed too. No one cares that I am exhausted," Mama screamed each time Daddy tried to talk to her about seeing Dr. Jones.

## Seven, No More

Sometimes at night, he would wake up to find her with a faraway, sad look on her face, still rocking Jim Boy, who was fast asleep. Mama's depression and anxiety were getting worse; she could not sleep. The lack of sleep and rest caused extreme fatigue. Daddy knew something had to be done now.

Next Saturday he insisted she come with him to see Dr. Jones. After the blood work was finished, the doctor talked to Mama about her condition, her depression, her anxiety and fears. After listening he suggested hormone therapy. At first she resisted, but then she decided Dr. Jones might be right. She would try it for a while. Dr. Jones gave her sample pills for two weeks thinking it might be a hardship for them to buy the medicine. In a couple of weeks, the family noticed a big difference. She was almost her old self. Mama continued with the hormone therapy.

Dr. Jones knew what to do!

# New House! New Beginnings!

Later that fall after the cotton was harvested, Daddy told about a house one block from his work. The house was for lease or sale. "Would you like to see the house Sunday afternoon? I don't know about the price of the house, but let me find out," he said to everyone.

Mama hesitated, wondering if she would like the big city, but later realized it might be the best for Daddy, the children, and maybe her.

"Yes, we want to see the house," the children shouted together. So on Sunday after church, all seven children, Mama, and Daddy piled into Miss Susie: Daddy driving and Mama holding Jim Boy in the front seat, Anna Grace holding Sara Beth, with Ellie Mae, Billy Bob, and Lilly Lee on the back seat, and Holly Rose holding down the hump. Everyone was going to the big city to see "The House."

On the way to see the house, Mama said, "This house sounds too good to be true. Can you imagine two toilets?

## Seven, No More

Plus all the bedrooms and within walking distance to just about everything we need."

Daddy replied with pride in his voice, "Yes, but, Mama, in the city, the toilets are called bathrooms."

Anna Grace asked, "Could we take a bath every day, since they have a bathtub with hot and cold water?"

Ellie Mae said, "Why would you need to take a full bath every day, just because we have a bathtub in the house? Now we take a full bath once a week. We don't get that dirty, Anna Grace. If we wash our hair every day, it will lose its body and we'll look like some of those city girls with straight stringy hair."

Holly Rose and Sara Beth were thrilled at the thought of a bathtub in the house. Maybe the two of them could learn to swim at the same time when they were bathing. The only difference Holly Rose saw between the two was that swimming, they needed a swimsuit; taking a bath, they were naked.

Listening to the girls, Billy Bob was thinking and forming his own opinion about the bathtub. With Billy Bob being quiet, Ellie Mae knew he was thinking about fishing, but she didn't say anything. Since Ellie Mae was the talker in the family, it was most unusual for her to be quiet. Lilly Lee was having trouble understanding what the problem was about the bathtub. She knew Mama wouldn't let Billy Bob put fish in the tub. By the time all of them had a bath every day, they would probably use all the water coming to the house.

As they arrived at the big house, Daddy parked Miss Susie in the driveway. Opening the doors, they piled out like cattle in a herd following the leader. While Daddy opened the door to the house, Billy Bob and Lilly Lee went running around outside.

*Marlene Rose*

Into the backyard they went. Lilly Lee found a clothesline just like what they had at home. Billy Bob found a doghouse with a fence around it.

"I guess we can bring old Harvey. He won't run away like he does back home," Billy Bob said, excited about finding the doghouse.

Then all the children went into the house, each one claiming a bedroom. The house had four bedrooms, a toilet on the back porch with a bathtub, plus an additional toilet with a bathtub in the middle of the house. Daddy informed them again that in the city the toilets are called "bathrooms." After looking at the house, they were so excited.

After looking at the size of the house, Anna Grace thought this must be how the rich live. Within a block of the house was a general store that also had a soda fountain. Did they have enough money to buy the house?

The next day, Monday, Daddy met the owner at the house on his lunch hour. Using all his time after he ate, he didn't have time to read to Dwight, but Dwight understood. The owner assured Daddy that the Federal Housing Authority would loan him the money with his salary. Within the first year of employment, he was made foreman of several men—one of them being Dwight. Daddy applied for a loan on the house and was approved. After closing, they had money left over. Now they owned their own house!

Upon arriving home after buying the house, Daddy told the family he wanted to see his friend, Mr. Weathers. With excitement and sadness Daddy and Billy Bob told Mr. Weathers about the family moving to the big city. Daddy thanked Mr. Weathers for being such a wonderful friend and neighbor for the past four years, saying to him, "With you loaning us farm equipment; helping Billy Bob on his pro-

## Seven, No More

jects, like making the sled; caring for the children when Anna Grace was sick and hospitalized; and giving us the inner tubes when it snowed, we can never thank you enough."

Billy Bob said, "Daddy, remember Mr. Weathers loaned us the angel for the Christmas tree."

Daddy replied, "We will miss having you come to eat with us on Sundays and special occasions. Just maybe you can find your way to visit us."

Mr. Weathers just stared at both of them. He did not believe what he heard. Sadly he turned away without saying anything.

On the way back home across the field Billy Bob looked up at Daddy, saying, "It will be a sad day when we leave Mr. Weathers and Big Black Dog."

After hearing Billy Bob and his family were moving to the big city in less than a month, Mr. Weathers started thinking and planning something special for his friends. Talking with Granny, Mr. Weathers decided to give his friends and all their friends a barbecue.

Granny and Mr. Weathers contacted Grandma and Mr. Farris about helping with the plans for the barbecue party. Mr. Farris donated a hundred-pound dressed pig from his grocery store. Granny helped inviting the guests. She invited their friends from their church and their friends from the mill village where they once lived. Mr. Weathers set the date: it would be the first Saturday in November. Mr. Weathers told Granny, "Let's have an old-fashioned barbecue like we used to have twenty years ago. My mama could fix the best potato salad, slaw, hush puppies, and lemonade in the world."

Granny looked at him and said, "We will get every one to make their favorite dish for the barbecue. Is that all right?"

Without answering, Mr. Weathers just shook his head

*Marlene Rose*

yes. On the day of the barbecue Mr. Johnson, Daddy's friend from church, Daddy, and Mr. Weathers dug the pit to cook the pig. In amazement, Billy Bob stood and watched them dig and fix the pit. The pit was to be twelve inches deep, six feet long, and three feet wide with metal rods across the pit supporting the pig as it cooked—turning the pig one time during the cooking. Beside the pit, they laid a piece of old tin that Mr. Weathers had laying around his yard. They built a fire with oak wood on the tin, and as the oak wood burned, it became red hot coals. One of the men shoveled the hot coals under the cooking pig. This method of cooking continued until the dressed pig was cooked. This cooking took about eight hours with continuous brushing of homemade barbecue sauce, using Mr. Weathers's recipe for the sauce. He wouldn't give that recipe to anyone. It was a family secret. Not knowing each other before, Mr. Weathers and Mr. Johnson became well acquainted by the end of the day. The two of them talked about all the good times with the family and drank Mama's sweet ice tea.

While the pig was cooking, Mama, Granny, and Grandma were preparing the other foods and drinks, with the exception of the lemonade.

Mr. Weathers made the lemonade in a big wooden tub. The children hoped he didn't wash his clothes in that tub. He assured everyone that that tub was just for lemonade. It had not been used in twenty years. Rolling each lemon until he felt the juice inside, Mr. Weathers would cut off the ends of each lemon, then squeeze the juice into the wooden tub. Next adding water and sugar to taste, he blended the three items together into a delightful lemonade in the wooden tub.

Grandma was thrilled at having a barbecue. She told Mr.

## Seven, No More

Weathers she would make the potato salad and the mixture for the hushpuppies. Grandma peeled and diced the potatoes, cooking them until they were fork tender. After the cooked potatoes were drained and cooled, she added diced onions and pickles with chopped hard-boiled eggs, folding all the ingredients together with a little mustard and mayonnaise, seasoned with salt and pepper to taste—the best cold potato salad for any barbecue pig. She started making the mixture for the hushpuppies, blending together corn meal and corn oil, self-rising flour and water. It was ready for the hot oil to fry the hushpuppies.

Everyone in the family was involved in the barbecue. Mama made her sweet ice tea that everyone loved, plus she made the cole slaw with shredded cabbage, carrots, and diced onions, blending the three vegetables together with a cold salad dressing. Mama always added a little sugar to the cole slaw for something extra in taste. Anna Grace and Ellie Mae were busy cleaning the tables.

Mr. Weathers said, "The tables were last used for hog killing time about five years ago."

Each girl used white clean rags to scrub them. They prepared the tables with napkins and silverware. Bringing out the salt and pepper shakers, Anna Grace made sure they had extra barbecue sauce on each table for those who liked their food hotter.

Granny was setting up a table with desserts. Aunt Grace brought her favorite banana pudding. Miss Mary Moore, their friend from the mill village, brought her famous chocolate cake. Granny brought her pecan pie and blueberry shortcake, while Mama put her old-fashioned bread pudding on the table. She hoped Mr. Weathers liked it as much that day as he did on Sundays at the house. Lilly Lee was eyeing

*Marlene Rose*

all those good sweets, especially Granny's pecan pie, while the two little ones—Sara Beth and Jim Boy—were running around like little wild Indians. Holly Rose was following behind Granny, wanting to help, but really she wanted to eat.

Just as the pig was finished cooking, their friends started coming for food and fellowship with the family. Dr. Jones came by for a brief chat and to eat. He couldn't stay long, because he was going to deliver a baby down the road.

All at once, Mama looked sad. Daddy saw the look and smiled at her, reassuring her that her family—all seven children plus him—loved her. She smiled back at him. Then he knew everything was all right. Preacher Jim and his family came. They bragged on the food and fellowship. "We need to do this more often," he said, then added, "but not to have our friends move away."

Pete and Sally loved all that good pig with its trimmings. Pete was anxiously waiting for dessert time. He saw the chocolate cake that Miss Mary Moore made. He had tasted her food before and knew it was delicious.

Grandma and Mr. Farris were busy keeping the tables full of food, while Mama was busy pouring tea and lemonade. Mr. Weathers was looking around at everyone—half sad and half happy. He was going to miss this family, especially his buddy Billy Bob. Not forgetting Big Black Dog, Billy Bob carried him the scrap leftovers.

With all of this taking place in the first week in November, the lease on the land ended the first of December. Daddy told Mama and the children he wanted to paint the inside of the new house before they moved into it. "After work, Dwight and I can paint the house in two weeks," he said with pride in his voice.

Every day he drove Miss Susie to her new parking place

*Seven, No More*

in the driveway of their new house. Miss Susie liked being protected by the trees around the house and driveway. After work, Daddy and Dwight walked to the little store around the corner from the foundry to eat a sandwich; then they would start painting. Dwight was so appreciative. No one ever took time to read to him but Daddy.

He called Daddy his "cigarette-smoking, Bible-reading preacher." Mama thought he was trying to make points with Daddy because Daddy was Dwight's boss.

Daddy said, "Mama, don't you worry as long as I can get the word into him. I remember how much I wanted to help Mama with reading. She never learned to read, but she listened." As Daddy read the Bible, Dwight would listen. Often he would repeat to Daddy what he learned from him.

When Dwight found out they were moving during the Thanksgiving holidays, he offered to help. Daddy said, "Dwight is strong as an ox, and you can count on him doing a good job."

Two of Daddy's church friends also offered to help. One of them, Mr. Edwards, had a 1949 green Ford truck, plus Pastor Jim loaned Daddy his 1950 Chevy truck.

Mr. Edwards was about forty years old with three children of his own—about Anna Grace, Ellie Mae, and Billy Bob's ages. Mr. Edwards had straight black hair slicked down with Vitalis hair tonic and a Clark Gable mustache, with a sassy smile, according to Mama. He was one of Daddy's church friends, but Mama told Daddy, "I don't want you going off with him. He's a real ladies' man, and I know one when I see one."

Daddy's other buddy was Mr. Johnson, a nice laid-back, bald-headed fellow who was always kissing and hugging the

*Marlene Rose*

women, but Daddy said, "Look at his muscles. He and Dwight together could lift anything we have."

Mr. Johnson was older than anyone else in the crowd. He was to drive Pastor Jim's truck. Daddy didn't trust Mama to drive Miss Susie because she still didn't have a license. With the two trucks loaded and tied down and the car loaded with children; they were on their way to the big city with Daddy. Miss Susie led the caravan. Everything they owned was on those two trucks, so Mama didn't want them lost in the city.

As they were nearing the house, they saw a lot of people standing around with signs. "What in the world is going on?" Daddy asked.

Then he realized these people were from the foundry. Dwight must have told them that Saturday after Thanksgiving was moving day. Everyone discarded their signs and began carrying all the furniture inside the house. Mama didn't have to lift one piece of furniture. She didn't need to either. All the furniture was in place in the house late that afternoon. *No wonder Daddy loves those people at work,* she thought. *You couldn't ask for nicer people.* Afterwards, Mr. Edwards in his green truck and Mr. Johnson in Pastor Jim's truck left for home.

Daddy said, "I am starving!"

All at once, pulling up in front of the house was a school bus that had been turned into a van. It was painted red with white racing stripes. Out stepped the wives and children of Daddy's coworkers, carrying boxes of food for everyone. The children met one another, and Sara Beth announced, "This is going to be our best move ever. Look at all our new friends."

Being exhausted from all the work, Daddy's friends left with their wives and children after they ate. Then Mama and Daddy looked around in the neighborhood. Nearby were

*Seven, No More*

schools, churches, grocery markets, and a new shopping center being built. All were in walking distance from their new home. Miss Susie could get some much-needed rest after traveling thirty miles twice a day. She loved her new parking space in the driveway under the shade tree.

Billy Bob said, "I will miss Mr. Weathers and Big Black Dog." He and Daddy would miss their old fishing holes at the Neuse River, but they could find new fishing places. "When Jim Boy grows some, we'll take him with us!"

Lilly Lee said, "I am going to miss Granny helping me learn the guitar."

Then Mama injected, "Granny can come and visit for a while. Maybe she can catch you up with your lessons if you practice every day."

Holly Rose and Sara Beth were busy playing together. They probably wouldn't miss anything or anyone. They had each other!

Anna Grace and Ellie Mae were going to miss their friends at school, but they were looking forward to new friends and new challenges.

Mama said she was going to miss her family, but not enough to go back. Everyone was going to miss Dr. Jones. He could do anything!

They were happy in their new home!

NOV 0 9 2005
WA
18.95
3.00

ROSE

## DATE DUE

| | |
|---|---|
| DEC 0 2 2005 | |
| DEC 2 0 2005 | |
| DEC 2 9 2005 | |
| FEB 1 1 2006 | |
| FEB 1 6 2006 | |
| MAR 0 9 2006 | |
| MAR 1 8 2006 | |
| JUN 1 2 2007 | |
| SEP 1 1 2008 | |
| 8/2/10 | |
| | |
| | |
| | |
| | |
| | |
| | |